HEADING NORTH

HEADING NORTH

Joseph Van Nurden

NORTH STAR PRESS OF ST. CLOUD, INC.
St. Cloud, Minnesota

Dedicated to my wife and to my son
Emily and Soren

ISBN: 0-87839-338-2
ISBN-13: 978-0-87839-338-1

First Edition, May 2009

Printed in the United States of America

Published by
North Star Press of St. Cloud, Inc.
P.O. Box 451
St. Cloud, Minnesota 56302

northstarpress.com

CHAPTER *1*

R amblin' Man" by Hank Williams is the greatest song of all time. That fact had echoed through my mind daily for nearly two years. The song grabbed me on my way to Shakopee for the first day of what was supposed to be a month-long assignment through a temp agency. I listened to the song the next day, and the next, until listening to it joined guzzling coffee in the creation of a new ritual during my hour-long commute to work every day for four weeks.

The month-long assignment was extended, and then I was hired on as a full-time employee. I stopped playing the song every morning, but it stayed toward the front of my mind; sometimes only a line or two would briefly grace my thoughts, and sometimes the whole song would repeat in my mind over and over again.

Wanderlust can come and go throughout the course of a life. In my case I remember it being present for around twenty-one years. I am not sure if it had affected me during the first four years of my life, although I am told that I was very active.

Spring was looking like it was around to stay. It was the first week of April, and the snow had almost all melted, even in Northern Minnesota. The temperature was hovering around freezing and even staying above it on a few nights. The woods were clear, and that made me anxious to get back to them. It had been a mild winter, but I had spent most of it indoors.

I had been working six, even seven days a week at my warehouse job all winter so I could save up as much money as possible. I had not been able to get outside that much during the course of the winter.

The city was too much for me; I needed to get away. Everywhere I went there were people. Concrete. Signs. Malls. Garbage. Nothing was built to last. There were simply too many people and not enough trees. I had grown up in the woods, and although I had now been in the city for seven years, it seemed to be getting harder for me the older I was.

I had always been somewhat of a loner, even when I was entertaining a houseful of guests, but I was becoming more and more of a hermit as I aged. What I wanted more than anything was to be left alone. Every time I went out into the backyard, it seemed that the neighbors sensed I was there. I could not escape, even in my own backyard. I felt as if I always had eyes on me. Television eyes. Eyes that stared out of their windows during commercial breaks, eyes imagining the drama and excitement happening next door to them. The forest was where I went to get away. I felt more comfortable, inspired, and at home camped out among the trees than anywhere.

Whenever I would talk to anyone from the cities about the woods, they would start talking about parks. I had been to every park and explored every nook and cranny within a forty-five-minute drive from my house in St. Paul more times than I could recall, and they were not what I was after. Southern Minnesota has a lot of parks, but going to a park with paved walkways and picnic tables every half-mile to experience the wilderness was like going to the zoo to see wildlife—not enough. Most of the parks were not worth taking any more time to reach than forty-five minutes, and the days were too short to get away except for on the weekends.

I started going out to the woods because I was not happy being in the city. I felt claustrophobic around all the people. I wanted to be able to walk out my door and hike in any direction without having to cut through backyards and jump over fences. I felt myself becoming boring. I could only go to so many parties, concerts, and museums—they all blended together. I was tired of people.

The boss at work was surprised when I requested to use five days of my vacation time. I had been working for the company for two years and had put in so many hours since starting that she had started to refer to one of the storage rooms I was in charge of as my bedroom. When I got home, I packed my frame pack with all of the necessary, and a lot of unnecessary, camping gear. I picked out a few books, maps, and a lot of music to keep me company and headed north to Chippewa National Forest to get some decent sleep in the woods.

I was taking a vacation not only because I needed to get away; I also wanted to take the time to really examine the goals I had set for myself and the dreams I held onto. I held a long-standing fantasy of getting away from the city forever. In my dreams I was camped out under pine trees two hundred feet tall, kayaking on lakes and rivers with only the sound of the loons breaking the silence, or hiking up hills, over creeks, and under a sky where only birds flew. After the long, hard winter indoors I had reached my mental breaking point with my life in the cities, and I had finally saved up enough money to make a clean break and live comfortably for at least a few years.

As I drove north on Interstate 35, I was again amazed by the sprawl of the city. I had done plenty of traveling in my life already and seen large cities. I had been to New York City, Chicago, Detroit, and Los Angeles, and I knew that the Twin Cities were not that big in comparison, but Minneapolis and St. Paul were too big for my taste. Every suburb was part of one big mess of car dealerships, strip malls, and warehouses. A lot of people born in the metro area did not consider outlying suburbs like North Branch to be part of the Twin Cities, but as an outsider I make no distinction.

Grand Rapids came into view at about 11:00 p.m. I stopped for gas. The cashier was talking to an elderly man as I walked in, but the man stepped aside and the cashier was courteous as I paid for my gas. As I started to walk away, the two of them resumed talking and invited me into their conversation. It was refreshing to be back.

The paper mill stood out—there was nothing else like it in town—but in the Twin Cities and suburbs, it would have been anonymous amongst the thousands of other similar buildings. It had sprung up in Grand Rapids right over the source of the town's namesake over one hundred years ago.

Highway 38 led me to where I would find a place to set up camp. I did not have to worry about any of the established campsites being taken in the beginning of April. Even in the summer most of the visitors to the area that came to camp went to the campgrounds, not to the dispersed sites that could be found throughout the forest.

I was on vacation in a National Forest. The way that people vacationed in the National Forest had changed considerably, even since the 1980s. When families came up to camp now they were bringing laptop computers, cell phones, and televisions with them. Seeing people sitting around watching televisions at the campgrounds made me think of trailer parks. More and more people could not go for a week without seeing what was going on with the rest of the world. People had to be entertained continuously; they could not sit and relax anymore. When I would mention camping in conversation, I was often asked what kind of camper I had, or if I had an RV.

The place I had in mind to start the week was about twenty miles north of Grand Rapids, but I knew it would be at least another hour before I would start to set up my camp because I still had to gather wood for a fire on the way there. I drove down a forest road and gathered up branches and logs from the side of the road and cut up two trees that had fallen over it so I would be sure to have enough for my fire

As I continued down the road I turned and drove up a spur that ended in a small clearing. The spot I ended up at seemed like a decent place to camp and it was already late, so I decided to sleep there instead of continuing on to the old tried and true site I originally planned on staying at.

I got a good fire going and realized I was getting hungry. I cooked some oatmeal and opened an ale. I laughed out loud to think of eating breakfast for my first meal—it was a new day, after all. The aurora borealis was very active overhead and after stringing up my hammock, I lay and looked up at the changing light display. An owl nearby kept me company as I watched the show. Around 3:00 a.m. I decided I should try to get some sleep. I built the fire up so it would not burn out for a few hours and wrapped myself up in a fleece sleeping bag, followed by a down bag and finally pulled a tarp around and tucked into my cocoon.

I woke up just after eight o'clock and crawled to my woodpile to get my fire going again. I got the coffee underway and wandered around my camp. I had made a mess getting unpacked. There were pots, pans, pieces of firewood, and articles of clothing spread out from the back of my truck to my fire. It looked like a bear had been in my camp.

When setting up a camp after dark, it always looks drastically different than it does when morning rolls around. The woods seem like a wall in the darkness, and it only opened up when I was wandering through it. Camps are never that closed off when it gets light out, especially before the leaves appear. I knew that the morning would change my camps. I liked to focus on the initial impression from the night, before the daylight took it.

I put water on to boil and made spaghetti for breakfast, I had my meals switched around on me, but I was on vacation and my goal was to break out of the routine I had been following. Breaking out of my routine was important. I was in control of my days. I did not have a list of necessary tasks for the day. I spent the rest of the day gathering more firewood and wandering through the forest. There were pockets of snow in the shadiest places, but mostly I found only bare ground.

The deer made very easy paths to follow where they traveled often. The paths were not always high enough for a person, so there was a lot of ducking and weaving through bushes involved. Deer paths meandered through the woods and along the lakes, and I followed them for a few miles and found two old deer stands.

As rotten as a lot of the old deer stands in the woods were getting, I still liked to climb them to see the vantage points. Permanent deer stands were not supposed to be built on National Forest land, but there were still a lot of them out there in the trees, and new stands were still being built. Only one collapsed on me. I was not hurt when it happened since I heard the wood cracking and prepared for the fall.

My camp was still waiting for me when I returned after dark. I built up my fire and scrambled some eggs. I did a little reading by the light of the fire and went to sleep with a few snowflakes in the air.

I woke up four hours later, and as I rolled out of the tarp and my sleeping bags it was snowing hard. It was still dark out, but I saw that my camp was covered in about four inches of snow already and was showing no sign of letting up. It had come down over an inch an hour. Snow had a tendency of sneaking up on me. I suppose part of why that always happened was that I never listened to the news or weather reports. It had not totally smothered my fire, so I was thankful for that, and I was glad that I had taken the time to dig out an extra tarp and covered my woodpile before I went to sleep and the flakes turned substantial. I threw more wood on the fire and crawled back into my cocoon for a few more hours of sleep.

When I woke up for the day, it was still snowing hard. I pulled a shovel out of the back of my truck and started to shovel snow out from around my truck and the camp. Things were not looking very promising.

I drove a small two-wheel drive, manual-transmission pickup truck. The truck got great gas mileage and was perfect for hauling my gear around, but it was not good at getting out of mishaps. I had saved up my money during high school and bought the truck in the eleventh grade, so I was very familiar with it. It took a few times getting seriously stuck to figure out how to control it. One of the positive things about the truck was how light it was. When I did get stuck, it was not that difficult to get out of mud holes and ditches.

I would have to find some heavy rocks to weigh down the back end of the truck so I would not spin out or get stuck in place. I knew where a few larger rocks were from my exploring the day before, and I had a few rocks that I had placed around my campfire. To be safe I cleared a decent sized area of snow so I could get turned around and get a good run at the road to get out.

After working at clearing away the snow and loading the rocks in the back of my truck, I thought about staying where I was for another day and heading out on snowshoes to do a bit of exploring. I decided to enjoy the fresh powder before it melted away and leave the next morning. I took the time to drive up and down the road a few times to pack the powder down to make sure I had a clear path when I left.

I went out walking and found the remains of a fresh wolf kill. A pack of wolves had made a feast of a deer. There was hair, bones, and blood covering the snow. I did not see any of the wolves around, but I knew it was very likely that they were just a little further up, watching me. As I followed the tracks a few hundred more yards, I could see where two of the sets of tracks had turned back toward the kill. They had been behind a stand of balsam, and I was sure that they had been watching me as I examined the remains of their feast. I followed the tracks for another mile and decided to start on my way back to camp.

The snow presented me with the opportunity to do something I had not planned on. I started rolling up snowballs and stacking them tightly, building walls around my camp. With all that I had to work with I was able to build myself a snow-fort large enough to sleep in. I added a few tunnels that I could store some of my extra firewood in. I had not built a fort in the snow in over fifteen years, and I still found it to be a lot of fun to do. It also did not take nearly as long to build a snow fort now. I slept well in the fort that night. When I woke up, it had finally stopped snowing. In all, at least a foot and a half of powder had come down.

I got the shovel back out and cleared my truck out again. I turned on my radio while I drank cold coffee. If the weather report was to be trusted, it sounded like the snow had been concentrated in a small area of the state. Fortunately, when listening to the weather report, the meteorologists were usually pretty accurate in describing what already happened, as opposed to what would happen; unfortunately the path of the storm included most of the area I was planning to tramp around in during my vacation time. I found out that farther north there was no snow to speak of, so I changed my plans and turned north. I drove to the terminus of Highway 38 in Effie and had a late dinner at the Effie Cafe.

The snow had everyone at the cafe riled up, and quite a few families had been snowed in. The plows had been out in full force, and anyone who owned one went out to help with the effort. Many who were out plowing had already detached their plows for the season, but they wasted no time putting them back on to plow out the driveways of their neighbors. There had been a lot of cars in the ditches, so the tow-trucks were also very busy.

I drove west on Highway 1 to Northome, where I stopped and bought five bags of kettle chips, a case of soda, and a twelve-pack of ale. After looking over the map to make my decision of where to go next, I decided to take Highway 72 heading north. I stopped in at Big Bog State Recreation Area and walked along the boardwalk over the peat bog. I had not been to the park before, and it was nice to be able to walk through a bog and not have to wear hip waders or get soaked. I drove through the campground there and was the only person around. I briefly contemplated staying at a campsite by the Tamarack River but decided to move on.

This land was fascinating, but certainly not an ideal place for human habitation. In 1892 the great expanse of bog in Northern Minnesota that I was traveling through was called "practically unfit for any purpose." In 1908 dredging operations started to make the land suitable for people settling there. Over 1,500 miles of trenches were dug out, but the bogs did not drain. The farmers that attempted to work the land were forced to relocate. As a result of the difficulty faced by the early settlers and environmental pressures the bogs represent the largest undeveloped wilderness area in the United States. The total area is around five hundred square miles of undeveloped land. I hoped that no one would figure out a way to move in there and exploit the land.

The sun was out and there was no snow on the ground. It was hard to imagine that I had started my morning in a foot and a half of fresh snow farther south. I was glad to run into the conditions at the bog. There was only one other car at the park until I was digging food out of the back of my truck, then two DNR rangers showed up and began unloading equipment for examining the peat.

I drove farther on toward Canada and found a place to set up camp along the Big Fork River. It felt good to stretch my legs and breathe in the clean air. I took out my guitar and played all of the Townes Van Zandt songs I knew and then wrote a few simple songs to play until I was ready to go to sleep.

The next morning I drove on to Carp Swamp Wildlife Management Area and hiked about ten miles on the Baudette-Norris trail. The trail was mostly clear of snow so I did not bother strapping my snowshoes on my pack. Black spruce and tamarack trees pushed toward the sky out of the brush. Every square inch of a bog could be infinitely different from the land around it, moss and brush gave everything a lush look, sometimes seeming impenetrable.

Humans were not the best-adapted animals to the conditions found in bogs, and snowmobile season was over so I knew that I would not be seeing anyone on my trek. The bog was dotted with sinkholes of indeterminable depth, some only a few inches deep, some opening up underneath a person and one could very quickly be up to the waist in water.

Walking in a bog forced a person to step very high. A hike through it could be just as strenuous as going up a mountain, so it was very good exercise. I imagined an exercise machine that simulated the bog-walking experience would have to have two separate foot-sized platforms a few feet off the floor that would suddenly shift to the side or drop a foot. I was not sure it would be too fun cleaning up afterward if the mud and dark-brown water were waiting underneath for every slip while a person was working out at home or in the gym.

The ground was still firm along the whole trail, and I made good time. A few weeks later it would be hard to walk through it without sinking and hiking the same distance would take almost twice as long.

I next stopped at Franz Jevne State Park and ate on the banks of the Rainy River. At only one hundred and eighteen acres, Franz Jevne is very small, but it preserves an important piece of Minnesota wilderness.

There was a lot of open water on the river and still plenty of deep snow to trudge through between the black spruce, white cedar, and jack pine around the park. Hundreds of large chunks of ice were breaking free from the bank and rushing over Long Sault rapids as I sat and watched. I contemplated sleeping at one of the established campsites in the park, but decided to save my money and found some nearby public land to set up camp.

Driving east on Highway 11, I found myself going very slowly as I stared out my window at the Rainy River. I realized I was only driving twenty-five miles per hour when a truck driver held down his horn behind me. I hit my right turn signal and eased onto the shoulder to a driveway so the truck could pass, I looked over at the driver sheepishly as he continued to honk his horn and show me some of the sign language that he knew—I did not understand all of it, but I was fluent enough to get the general idea.

I stopped at Manitou Rapids for a break and continued to be mesmerized by the rushing water. A pair of magpies kept me company while I read a few chapters. I continued through Indus and Loman, and then stopped where the Big Fork River dumped into the Rainy River. I went for a walk up the banks and retraced the route of the river in my mind. I had always been fascinated with rivers, and growing up the Big Fork River was the nearest—the Mississippi was a close second. I made dozens of small rafts that I floated down the river, imagining where they would end up. When I was on the banks of any of the rivers I had visited before I always looked to see if any rafts had washed up. I never found any though, only garbage. The terminus of the Little Fork River was very close to that of the Big Fork River, although the beginning of each was very far apart, in different counties.

I made my way to the town of Littlefork and went for a walk by the Little Fork River and through town. I took Highway 217 and stopped at the Rat Root River and drove through the town of Ray before getting to the Kabetogama Lake Visitor Center of Voyageurs National Park. The park was not very busy, although there were a few cars around. I wandered around the park marina and looked out over the still frozen lake. Kabetogama Lake was huge. I thought it must be a lot of fun to own a small houseboat like was pulled on the shore of the summer homes and resorts around the area. I got stuck in a large snowdrift at Chief Woodenfrog State Campground and had to dig my way down to what turned out to be a tar road so I could get enough traction to escape.

The Echo Bay trail got my blood pumping since there was still snow that I had to work against. I walked about ten feet from my truck before retrieving my snowshoes. There were plenty of deer around to startle as I walked along the bay; it looked like the deer helped to clear the trail more than hikers had since winter had come around.

Backpacking through the snow seemed like a good idea, so I left my truck behind and set out on the Kabash Trail. I was glad to have my snowshoes along, but there was also a lot of clear trail. The trail followed the shore of Kabetogama Lake for the most part, so I was constantly treated to a view of snow blowing over the ice and snowdrifts among the trees. I set up camp at Bowman Bay on Kabetogama Lake and enjoyed the stillness of the night.

I backtracked along the Rainy River the next day, heading west toward Baudette. I was getting very low on gas and when I got to the gas station in Birchdale that was inexplicably closed I gambled that I would be able to make it to Baudette on the fumes in my tank. I was wrong.

Six miles out of town, my truck was sputtering almost nonstop, and then it quit on me. I coasted to the side of the road and put on my hazard lights. Around a dozen vehicles stopped to see what the problem was, but no one had gas cans with them. I finally talked to two high- school-aged kids in a beat up old Chevy that said they would run home and bring me back some gas.

I shut off my hazards and had a snack while I waited. Fifteen minutes. A half an hour. Forty minutes. I did not want to flag anyone else down and have the kids go through the trouble of getting the gas for me and coming back only to have me gone when they arrived, but I was contemplating turning my hazards back on when they reappeared. I dumped in enough gas to make it to Baudette and gave them some money for their help and then was on my way again.

I had never run out of gas before and felt pretty stupid that I let it happen. I had not been resetting my trip meter after getting gas so I had the odometer keeping track of total mileage for my vacation. I apparently mixed up the numbers in my head after the last refueling. I would not let that happen again.

Zippel Bay State Park was my next stop. The park was on Lake of the Woods. I imagined the Northwest Angle hiding away from prying eyes. The angle was part of Canada by land, but it was officially part of the United States. There was a lady out walking her dog with her car, the leash through her station wagon window. The car crawled along as the dog trotted. It was not very cold out, and it seemed like such a ridiculous sight to see.

The park was almost entirely closed off. No ranger was present and from the lack of tracks in the snow it looked like I was the only person who had been in the park for a few days. I decided I would need to come back with a boat some day so I could tour Lake of the Woods and go out to Garden Island.

I drove south through Beltrami Island State Forest and explored a dozen forest roads. There were several pine plantations with trees around fifty or sixty years old. I put on over one hundred miles on the gravel roads as I made my way south toward Red Lake, and I only saw two other vehicles.

My camp for the night was in the Red Lake State Wildlife Management Area. I heated up water and washed up as well as I could, I was planning on spending a little time inside the next day so I could enjoy a hot meal indoors. I did not want to smell too offensive.

In the morning I continued south. I stopped for a burger and fries at The Hill in Squaw Lake. I stayed in my booth and read a book while I slowly worked at finishing off three pots of coffee. I had not been inside for so long since I had left my house. I drove along the Avenue of the Pines scenic byway and swung back north to Suomi Hills.

I hiked some of the north loop of the Suomi Hills trail and camped out for a night by Spruce Island Lake. There I built a lean-to out of popple and balsam boughs. It was a nice little shelter, and I kept the fire going hot enough to keep it warm throughout the night.

I stoked up the fire when I woke and put my coffeepot over the coals to start the day. I was preparing my breakfast when I began to notice a few snowflakes in the air.

I sat scrambling up a few eggs for a morning sandwich. As the first snowflakes fell I was eating my eggs and thinking about moose. I was camped out next to a marshy area I knew would be perfect for a moose to wander through, and I had not seen one in over a year. I had seen some tracks here and there crossing the snowmobile trails, and I had found some moose droppings, but did not even have a fleeting glimpse at the large ungulate. As I sat there, a large bull moose walked across the marsh less than fifty feet from where I sat.

I watched the bull as it slowly walked and grazed, then lay down. Not wishing to disturb the moose, I stayed where I was. After I finished my breakfast, I started reading my book, while keeping an eye on the bull. About an hour after the bull moose had come into view, two cow moose leisurely made their way out of the brush. I sat and watched the moose until they moved on and thought about the pace of life that I had been living at for years.

I had not taken the time to sit down without reading, listening to music, watching a movie, or talking on the phone in a very long time. There were times when the sound of passing automobiles and voices from other rooms drove me crazy. I always kept music or a movie on to neutralize the sounds. I was able to feel a semblance of control over the situation if I could create a sort of white noise to block out the disturbances.

In the age of the Internet I was not immune to instant gratification and taking part in a constant flow of information. The problem with all of the entertainment and information was that even though it was there, there was not enough time to absorb it all. The information that people did pick up on often seemed to be the inconsequential things.

I hiked the rest of the north loop that day as the snow kept falling and made my way to the Miller Lake washout to set up camp. The lake had disappeared overnight in 1993, all of the water rushing down into Amen Lake, leaving the former lake bottom open to exploration without scuba gear. As I was gathering firewood, I found a raccoon skull under some fallen logs, the rest of the skeleton was nowhere to be seen—of course the snow did not help my search.

I hiked the rest of the south loop of the Suomi Hills trail the next day. It was the last full day of vacation. I would have to drive back to the city so I could be back to work early Monday morning.

The next day I drove to Trout Lake and hiked a few miles before continuing on to Grand Rapids for coffee. It was hard to drive back to the cities. Of course I always had the weekends—but is that really enough?

Chapter 2

I gave my two weeks notice the day that I returned to work. When I got back to the city, things had changed. A week away from the city had been enough for me. I had proven to myself that I would be fine living in the woods. I just could not live there anymore. I told my roommates that I was leaving the house after living there for six years.

I had been working for exactly two years in a warehouse as a material handler. The warehouse manufactured and distributed medical equipment, but it was known best for the heart monitors made there.

It was not the type of work I aspired to as I was working my way through college, but I had originally been set up with the job through a temp agency, and I found that the work made my days go by quickly, and the pay was a lot higher than I could find anywhere else. I had a bachelor's degree in history from a private college with a decent reputation, but found that without going through graduate school it meant next to nothing on the job market.

When I got home from work, I did not have enough options. I could read a book. I could watch a movie. I could go on the Internet and send e-mails to people I had not physically seen in years. I could go out to eat in some restaurant, surrounded by strangers. I could go to the theater. I could go to see a band play somewhere. I could go and get drunk in a bar.

So many options, but they all seemed so limiting. None of them seemed to be any fun. They were not interesting to me. When I did any of those things I felt like a drone. I was not really living at all. I was being entertained. Pacified. I was not making my own way. I did not feel I was an interesting person in any way, and I grew bored when in conversations with others. If we sat around talking about the entertainment we had witnessed, I felt lonely.

The woods had always inspired me. To me the woods and wilderness meant I had a place to be, and I could be what I wanted to be. I always was attracted to wilderness themes and getting away from it all. I read a lot of books as I was growing up with similar themes. I always responded to the themes of making it on my own and being able to support myself. I was interested in the voyageurs, mountain men, cowboys, hoboes, the back-to-the-land movement, and modern-day travel as well. The stories were powerful enough to stay with me. As I went through the motions of my life, I realized that the stories made more sense to me than the way I was living. The world was filled with options, many of them only closed off due to lack of imagination.

One-hundred-four weeks. Four weeks off for vacation and sick time. Twelve days off for holidays. I had been in that warehouse between fifty and sixty hours a week, with many Saturdays and even a few Sundays thrown in.

If I had been career minded and wanted to stick with my field of study I could have sacrificed and began volunteering and slowly working my way into a permanent job, but I decided I wanted something else. I did not want a career, I wanted to enjoy every day of my life, I wanted to do things on my own terms, and if I had to sacrifice some of the niceties of civilization so I could live on my own, that did not seem unacceptable. I needed to find a way to get enough money saved up so I could escape the rat race. I was impatient though and did not want to wait. I could win the lottery or rob banks to get quick money, but neither seemed very likely.

Minnesota had a lot of smaller high-tech companies that paid decent wages, and I had a few friends who had found high-paying jobs in warehouses. I went the route that my friends had taken and signed up with a temp agency. When I first started at the warehouse, I could not imagine being there for any length of time, it just seemed too draining. The money was a lot better than I could find anywhere else though, and that was what I needed. The company was growing faster than new positions could be filled. There was plenty of overtime available at time and a half with the lack of workers. I worked a lot of twelve-hour days to build up my paychecks.

I had to keep reminding myself during those first few months that getting hired on was what I needed in order to follow through on my plans of dropping out. I knew I needed to keep working there after that first day because I needed to know that it was the wrong course for my life. I felt I had to have the experience of working a job I was not at all passionate about so I would not lose focus.

I wished that I could be happy working for someone else. I wanted to be comfortable being a drone because it would have made life a lot simpler. There were times when it was fine; just the fact that I was keeping busy helped to make the days go by quickly. Whenever I started to feel comfortable, I would imagine what my life would be like in five or ten years if I kept at it . . . and it was too overwhelming.

It was strange going into the work world. I had worked at ten different part-time jobs during college, and I would always quit when I got tired of them. I was used to things changing constantly, like with my college courses. Every semester I had different classes to attend and a different job to get bored with.

I could have tried to move into another position there, but I considered working out on the floor of the warehouse as being much more honest than working in a suit and bossing other people around or trying to sell products that I really could not care less about. I would have plenty of time to decide if it had been worth it if I followed through on my plans.

I had earned enough money on the job to pay back my college loans. I kept money in a bank account and took out enough in cash to last me for at least a year.

The job had not been bad, but I did not want to live the way that people in the city lived. The job was part of another way of life, one that seemed foreign to me even after being there for two years. I had a great health insurance plan, options for profit sharing and a 401k plan with company matching funds. I had all of the trappings I needed to settle into a little suburban home with a thirty-year mortgage and a brand new automobile bought through the dealer next door with my company discount. These were not things I wanted though.

I was relatively healthy, even with my health insurance paid for I had not been to the doctor in four years. When growing up in the woods no one I knew went to the doctor unless they had a broken leg or were lying at death's door. Health Insurance was something that I never even considered until I was in a Sociology course in college and the professor made a huge deal out of people not having health insurance.

I did not want to take on any debt for a home either. I did not want to be in one place for very long. There was too much to see. When I started seeing the things I wanted to through travel, I realized that I would be very busy if I went to all of the places that I wanted to go.

I felt that if I could not pay for something outright, it was not worth buying. This attitude about money seemed to put me at odds with everyone I met in the city. Many people I worked with were continuously checking their credit scores and looking to trade in their vehicles before they had even reached the end of their payments.

As my co-workers had approached me over the two weeks since I had given my notice, the majority of them expressed a sort of envy that I was getting out. They did not understand what I was going to do. It seemed very foreign, but it also seemed right to them. I did not say much about my reasons for leaving other than that I planned to travel. Many of them said they wished they could do it. People I had known for two years confessed that they often dreamed of leaving everything behind—their houses and cars and jobs. Was I really so strange?

The fact that I was leaving gave my co-workers someone to confess to, and I was encouraged by everyone to live my new life to the fullest. I was surprised by some of the people who voiced opinions similar to my own.

It did not seem like anyone who worked their lives away to buy new cars, boats, houses, and all of the fixes never really had time to enjoy the things they worked so hard to be able to purchase.

How had others done it? How could all of my co-workers keep at it for all of the time they already had? Some of them had been with the company for fifteen years. It shook my perceptions of humanity. To think about all of those people returning day after day, week after week, and month after month until they looked up and realized they had spent a decade or more living paycheck to paycheck to pay off interest on loans and credit card debt. There were plenty of people who fought for careers while not having anything to show for it, or not having the time to enjoy what they had to show for it. Consumerism, and what people gave up to have more stuff, was astonishing to me.

I thought about the millions of people in the United States who would have felt privileged to have the job and the wages that I did, that I was giving up to live out of my truck and to sleep on the ground, and I laughed.

Gas, food, and new books once in a while were all I really needed. I did not need that much money to get by, and I had been saving every spare cent I could for two years. I had been living in the same house with the same four friends since my sophomore year of college. The house had been owned by the parents of one of the other occupants, and we were living there nearly free of charge.

It had been very trying for me to stay in that house while I finished up college and started at my job. I had to tell myself every morning when I woke up that it was for my future benefit to keep at it. The time was finally at hand.

Except for an unforeseen disaster, I could maintain my portion of the new world I was moving into. I was familiar with every nut and bolt in my truck. I had worked hard for it and still was proud to own it. It would be my home and I would have to be able to maintain it. Now that I thought about it, I'd owned my own home since I was seventeen years old; that was quite the accomplishment for a young man.

With a collection of several hundred books, a guitar, and plenty of pens and notebooks, I was certain I could stay plenty busy for the years to come.

I purchased field guides for every subject I could think of: mammals, birds, insects, edible plants, trees, weather, rocks, flowers, mushrooms, as well as survival books, maps, atlases, and foraging guides. I was sufficiently convinced that I had references for everything I needed to know about the world around me. There was no answer I could not find in my personal library.

I was equipped with all the camping gear I would need: cooking utensils, rifle, bow, fishing gear, kayak, and propane stove. I had a hammock, a cot, a camp chair, an air mattress, and tools—axe, hatchet, hammer, saws, and bolt-cutters. As I looked at it all piled up in my bedroom, I thought to myself that I might have overdone it, but I had plenty of space in the back of my truck for everything on my checklist. I had been slowly giving away the things that I would not need to my roommates and friends, who were more than willing to be showered with gifts from my overcrowded dwelling space.

With all my possessions already boxed and bagged, I loaded up my truck when I got home from work. I said good-bye to my roommates. I had lived there for six years and it was hard to leave—they convinced me to stay for supper although nothing elaborate was planned. We ordered pizza. They said they would come up to visit sometimes and a thousand-minute pre-paid calling card was one of my going-away presents.

While we were waiting for our pizza, cars began to pull up in front of the house. As Ashley, James, and Ryan walked in the door, I knew that I would not be able to leave right away. My friends had planned a party to keep me around for one more night, the sneaky devils.

I finally left at about 11:00 p.m. after those not too drunk went home, and those too drunk snored where they had passed out. I drove up Interstate 35 to Moose Lake, and came through Floodwood, then followed Highway 2 to Grand Rapids, and finally was in my new backyard when I drove up Highway 38 into the Chippewa National Forest and my new home. I drove up an old logging road that I had been on many times to a familiar campsite. I was a bit disappointed that my snow-fort was almost completely melted though.

The Chippewa National Forest contained 660,000 acres of land, all of which was open for camping. There were 280 already established 'dispersed camping' sites in the national forest. Each site had a small sign that said camping was free but there was a fourteen-day limit at each site. Many of the sites had campfire rings with cooking grates, and often an open pit toilet. There were sometimes even benches or picnic tables at the sites. If I stayed the limit at each site without ever going back I would be able to live in that particular forest for over ten years.

As I laid looking up at the stars and my frozen breath mingling with the smoke from my fire and rising toward them I thought about people in the city complaining when their furnaces or air conditioners stop working and they are forced to put on a sweater, and I laughed.

CHAPTER
3

I had always lived at a different pace from everyone around me. I needed time for just me. In a house full of roommates I had to get away for at least a few hours every day. I would go to a private study room in the library or lock myself in my bedroom for half the day with my headphones on. I needed time to recharge because being around people wore me out.

It was a beautiful night that first night I set up camp, although technically it was already morning. I hung my hammock between two trees, gathered wood from a few downed ash and balsam trees and started a campfire. I cooked up a can of beans and scrambled some eggs. The stars were out and I looked up at all of them and said aloud the constellations I remembered.

I thought of all I had left behind. Fourteen hours before I had been inside a heated warehouse. I had been living comfortably. Now I was on my own. Within a matter of hours, I felt as though everything that came before was a dream—of course the ale helped that along.

I had grown up in the area, and had lived and worked at a small family resort that my parents owned and operated until I moved to the Twin Cities for college. They had moved up and started the resort with next to nothing and became successful after years of hard work.

When they first took over the resort, families would come up for a week, and the fire ring would see bonfires every night. All of the guests would come out of the cabins and get to know each other. Some of the guests would bring guitars or tell stories. Every day during the summer there were new kids to meet, and every night I could go and listen to ghost stories, music, or play games.

Things started to change in the mid 1990s. The Internet started gaining in popularity and vacations began to change. Flights were cheaper so now every family could go to Disneyworld, and there were hotels with waterslides springing up around the cities. Keeping up with the Joneses seemed to catch up with everyone but the old-timers, but even they were affected. Working families were putting in more time at their jobs and did not seem to be able to leave for as long. Kids were more interested in video games and television now too. They would get there and look for a place to plug in their DVD players. Families would come and spend the day inside their cabins. Kids were showing up now and talking about other states, theme parks, and even other countries.

Parents wanted to be entertained the whole time they were on vacation as well. Bonfires just didn't cut it, and there were some groups that would go a whole week without saying hello to any of the other guests. It was becoming increasingly rare to have a family go out fishing everyday. The men didn't know how to fish, and they got fed up with waiting if they were not pulling something in every five minutes.

Guests began to show up with huge boats and motors, and we had to build bigger docks. It was evident from talking to our guests that the big trucks and boats they were bringing up made life tougher on them. They were stuck working to pay for something that was rarely used. When the owners of the monster boats actually brought them anywhere to use, they were nearly always upset because, even with $20,000 boats, they still did not know how to fish.

The guests ended up going out to eat as often as they could and going to the movie theater, golf courses, or anywhere that would keep them busy. It was sad that families could not relax. My parents had put the resort up for sale and moved to Colorado once my brother and I left.

I stayed in St. Paul after I finished with school to work and save my money. I still went up north at least once or twice a month to see old friends and to go camping. Slowly my friends moved away, so it got to be that there were only a few left. Now that I lived up north again, I had all my memories from growing up there, but I was not really connected with the area. I had worked or gone to school nearly every day I had lived there. It was only when I went back to visit and did not have to depend on a paycheck that I really could enjoy it. I thought it was a shame that I had to move away to really see how great it was where I had grown up, but I was glad I was finally able to really see it.

It was not easy to make a living in the area. People who stuck it out often worked seasonally and would take any extra job that came their way. There was wood to be cut and split, carpentry, masonry, wiring, mowing, haying, landscaping, snowplowing, trapping, deliveries, road grading, surveying, burning, school buses to be driven, and music to be played. I would often find men and women who it seemed had and were able to do just about any sort of work I could think of.

The area was very poor financially, but it was very rich in what mattered to me. It was an amazing place to live. Itasca County has over one thousand lakes, billions of trees, wildlife, and some of the most interesting humans a person was likely to meet anywhere.

The temperature dropped considerably during the night. I woke up shivering a few hours after tucking in for the night. My fire was only giving off faint wisps of smoke. I threw a few balsam boughs onto the fire and hopped up and down as the fire crackled back to life. I added a few chunks of wood and dug a coffee can out of my pack along with my percolator.

As I waited for my coffee to boil, I pulled out my watch: 7:36; twenty-four hours before I had been getting out of the shower, my coffee waiting for me on the counter in the kitchen, and I had tossed a few slices of leftover pizza into the microwave for breakfast. This morning could not be more different, I thought.

As my fingers warmed up around my tin cup, I looked out at the frozen lake. It had been a mild winter, and there was only snow left in some of the shady pockets of the forest. I watched a deer cross the lake and listened to the ravens making their observations.

After breakfast I walked around the lake, examining my new front yard. I paused often to note the stillness of the air and the profound silence. From my former front yard, I could hear automobile noises, televisions, stereos, and human voices at all hours of the day and night. Here there were only the ravens and black-capped chickadees. I would have to strain my ears to birds above the din of the city sounds, but here the bird songs seemed almost deafening amidst the leafless trees and patches of snow. One of the tree branches made me think of a pterodactyl sweeping low over the ground as my view of it flickered with the fire.

When I was in the first and second grades, my brother, a friend, and I had plans to build a time machine. My uncle had given me a book on dinosaurs that I was fascinated with. I brought the book with me on the bus and would often look through it. There was an old dump on our property filled with old household and industrial appliances. There were plenty of unrecognizable pieces of rusty metal there for us to practice our welding skills with before the real construction started. Our plan was to collect those scraps and weld them together in my dad's garage to create the structure for our contraption. After we had the structure of our time machine built we would install the controls and the computers that would transport us. The next step was to figure out how to get our contraption back through time.

In order to build the time machine we needed the parts. We saved computer chips and pieces of radios and televisions, figuring they would come in useful once we started to put everything together. We asked everyone for whatever spare electrical components they could help us out with, whether it was old transistor radios, tape decks, or remote-controlled cars, and the collection continued to grow. We never did let any adults in on our plans—it was probably the first secret I had. There was an older kid on the school bus that read a lot of science fiction. He began talking about dinosaurs one day, and we let him in on our plans. We asked what he knew of time travel, and he threw out a bunch of big words. I took extensive notes and followed up on them through the library at school. Unfortunately we never got the time machine figured out, and we gave up on it when

Teenage Mutant Ninja Turtles started to come around. Then we started to look into karate and skateboarding. I still had the book, packed away in the back of my truck, although the pages were smeared and falling out.

That night I bedded down after playing a few songs on my guitar. I had first started playing the guitar ten years before, although I only rarely picked it up to learn new songs. I had been in a few bands when I was younger, but had never taken it that seriously. At my house during college, some friends and I used to play down in the basement, but since I started working I did not have time to play much. I had spent most of my spare time at parties, or hiding in my room reading. The few two-day stretches that I had off from work were used for traveling around the state and finding new places to hike, kayak and camp. That was all different now. I did not have anywhere to be in the morning, or for any morning in the foreseeable future

CHAPTER
4

The nights and early mornings were still fairly chilly when I moved up north. I was spending a lot of time gathering firewood, and it seemed that I was burning it all up just as quickly as I gathered it. It was very different living out of doors. My body adjusted to being outside all of the time, although I always kept several layers on.

After changing camp a few times, I began to get into a routine. I quickly learned what I needed to do every day. If I skipped something I could tell later when I was rained on, the wood was almost gone, I had critters in my camp, or if I could not find what I was looking for. When I first moved up north, I was not sure how things would be living outside during the month of April in Northern Minnesota. I was still not sure how the next April would be even after staying through the first.

The months could be very different from one year to the next, so I had to be prepared. I had camped in the snow quite a few times before, but for the most part it was only for a day or two at a time. My vacation had prepared me for what I would be living with, and I always had places I could go if it simply got too cold or inhospitable in the woods. If I had not worked so hard at gathering firewood and finding campsites where I could be sheltered from the elements, things could have been a lot worse, and I may have given up. After the snowstorm had hit during my vacation, I was reminded that anything could happen with the weather and it would always be colder in the woods than it was in the Cities.

While it was true that I was not forced to flee indoors when it got cold out, I still could not do as much when I could see my breath twenty-four hours of the day. I took out my guitar and sang songs to the trees and owls at night. I could never write anything as beautiful as the sound of the branches swaying, punctuated by the hoots of owls out on the prowl for their nocturnal feasts, but they inspired me to try harder. The temperature had been going from one extreme to another during the end of April and May. Some nights I ended up wearing six layers to keep my teeth from chattering, and I was already sleeping with two sleeping bags.

Gathering firewood was an essential chore every day, no matter the time of year. Wood was available everywhere, but farther away from the most popular campsites were places with enough downed trees to supply firewood for a year. I was spending a lot of time getting firewood together when I came up, since the nights were still very cold, and would remain so until at least the middle of May. I needed to gather wood for about four hours to have a decent fire going throughout the night. As it warmed up, I let the fire die down while I slept and I just pulled the sleeping bags tighter together, or wore more clothing. I still was waking up cold when I had to add more wood to the fire, but I got used to it.

What I considered acceptable as firewood was changing continually, of course this had a lot to do with availability. I always gathered the most recent dead and downed trees first, but after a day in camp there would be a lot more rotten wood found in my piles, I figured I might as well clear that stuff out before I took the other wood. I am not sure how much I affected the forest by taking some of the nutrients away from it, but I figured that with all of the ash and heat I was creating that some pines might eventually pop up where I had been rather than popple. Pine need fire to come through sometimes to clear the duff away and provide nutrients for new seeds to take root and produce healthy trees. Jack pine cones need a short burst of heat to open up and drop seeds.

Occasionally I wished that I owned a chainsaw because it would save me a lot of time, but I wanted to do it all by hand. It suited me better to use my bow saw. I did not need to draw attention to where I was camped out, and the exercise got the blood flowing, and I felt better when I was done with the work. When I first started cutting up firewood, I was splitting it into several pieces, but it burned a lot longer if left whole, so I would only split a few pieces up every day so I had enough kindling to get the fire going.

I had grown up feeding a woodstove from October through April and cutting down trees and splitting firewood the rest of the year. Balsam and popple were the trees of choice for firewood, mostly because of the availability of them and especially popple because it grew fast and it was a less desirable tree to have around. The balsam were often very hard to split. Branches shot out in all directions, and the knot structure was sometimes next to impossible to split through; the grain of the wood was interrupted every inch or two by the swelling around the knots. Some of the balsam seemed to contain about a gallon of sap for every two or three board feet, and balsam sap is the stickiest I have encountered, although that probably has a lot to do with how much is present in the wood as compared to other species. Balsam is covered in what look like blisters entirely filled with sap. When burning balsam, our chimney had to be cleared often also, the creosote buildup could start chimney fires and lead to lost homes.

Firewood for the woodstove had to be a much higher quality than needed for campfires. Rotten wood was not fit for burning in a woodstove. It made a mess, and the amount of ash it produced versus the heat it gave off was not really worth bringing it inside. Another problem with rotten wood was that it was often the home of ant colonies. The colonies froze up in the winter and the ants went into a sort of hibernation, but when the wood heated up in the spring or when it warmed in the house, the ants came pouring out.

Campfires were a suitable place to burn any sort of wood. Sticks, roots, and rotting logs were all welcome in my fires for the heat and light they provided, although once the wood was to the point of squishing underfoot rather than cracking, I always left it for the forest floor to absorb.

Balsam boughs and birch bark were the best things to use for starting fires and spreading out the flames as they flared up. Small sticks and finely split wood made good kindling, and a few decent logs, once burning would provide the heat I needed. Over time, I grew much better at lighting fires. Fewer matches used, less frustration, and fewer frozen digits and limbs were the reward for learning to light wet wood and properly building a fire.

Dropping trees was invigorating but also very dangerous. Several people I knew had cut themselves very badly with chainsaws. Those that came away from a chainsaw accident with scars as the only result were fortunate it wasn't worse, and they typically would not allow it to happen to them again. Chainsaws started to kick back on the user when the teeth got dull or when knots were hit. Hidden hazards when cutting down trees included nails, spikes, screws, barbed wire, bullets, rocks, and even chains that were sometimes discovered in trees. These are often not visible, but when they are nicked with a chainsaw, they can be deadly. Unfortunately even a serious problem was not always evident while examining trees. At one time a tree could have supported a deer stand, had signs nailed to them, been hit by bullets or served as makeshift fence posts and strung with barbed wire that had long since eroded, except inside the wood.

Another danger facing any sawyer cutting down trees for firewood, logs, or boards were the widowmakers, dead limbs and treetops that can break loose and plummet to the earth. Widowmakers were especially common in birch trees. The first part to wither and turn brittle was the top of the tree, so in an otherwise healthy looking tree there could still be a widowmaker waiting for the unsuspecting sawyer. Sadly, one of my cousins was killed by a falling widowmaker; the dead top had snagged momentarily in another tree as it fell, and then came crashing down at an unnatural angle as the branches that held it in place snapped.

Agropelters are one of the most dangerous creatures in the forest. They are one of the many mythical creatures that the lumberjacks and voyageurs had to deal with as they worked in the wilderness. The agropelters live in the tops of trees and throw branches and treetops down at unsuspecting sawyers as they fell trees. They occasionally perform their nasty deeds on unwary hikers and campers as well. Agropelters are responsible for thousands of deaths throughout the long and storied history of logging.

Felling trees with the proper precautions, knowledge, and experience was much safer than it appeared. An experienced sawyer became adept at spotting snags and other dangers from terrain and equipment and learned how to drop a tree exactly where it would cause the least damage and avoid them falling into other trees and getting hung up. Hung up trees caused frustration, and frustration often led to carelessness. Taking the time to undercut the trees—cutting notches on the side where the tree should fall—and to note any warning signs, such as spotting top-heavy trees or those that would be pulled off balance by gravity with uneven branches, would result in the tree dropping safely.

I spent a lot of time reading and playing my guitar as the nights began to get warm. I took out my sketchbook and tried my hand at drawing the forest around me, but I decided I would rather just take a picture and go for a hike than spend an afternoon sketching trees.

Once the ice broke up, I was able to take my kayak out exploring. I went out first on North Star Lake. Ice still covered the center of the lake because of the depth there, but the edge of the lake was open enough to explore. I worked my way through the ice and pried sheets apart with my paddle here and there to help hasten the break up.

The loons were already back and ready for the temperature to start coming up. Their calls had been fascinating me for over a week. I watched them diving. They had to swallow some of the sand from the bottom of the lake first to aid in their digestion. I followed a pair along the shore and through a channel until I was near Wildcat Island. Whenever I see loons on a lake it was a certainty that the water was fairly clear. The loons tended to homestead the clearest lakes first so they could more easily see their meals below them.

No one had their docks in for the summer yet, and most of the homes along the lakeshores were still vacant. The summer-home owners sometimes would not see their own place for more than a weekend out of the year. Some years they did not even make it up at all.

Since there had not been much snow the previous winter, some of the creeks were shallow to start out with. A lot of rain would be needed if

I were going to follow all of the water trails that I had planned. Many of the creeks were choked with fallen trees, and there were many rocks jutting above the water. Not easy travel.

I had started kayaking the previous summer, but I had been hooked before I ever tried it. I loved being on the water and canoeing already, but the maneuverability and portability of kayaks was much more appealing. When I bought my first kayak, I shopped around and waited to actually purchase it until I had a beautiful weekend forecasted so I could have a whole weekend to spend with my new toy.

I think that the river raft race in the cartoon "Race for your life, Charlie Brown" was the biggest inspiration I had to get out on the water. My brother and I would each grab a laundry basket to sit in and pretend we were on the water while we watched the progression of Snoopy and Woodstock. I followed the progression in watercraft of inflatable alligator, to inner tube, to canoe, and finally I got a kayak. Canoes could not go all of the places that a kayak can. I owned a ten-foot kayak and a seven-and-a-half-foot-long paddle, it was a compact set up that I could just throw in the back of my truck and be ready to take off to wherever I was going. With my gear and supplies along, I usually was not dealing with a load over sixty five pounds when I would have to portage to different lakes or around blown-down trees and beaver dams.

I was able to start exploring many of the places I had only seen on my maps, and I found many places not on the map. It may sound odd, but I found it refreshing to be in a place where the maps were not accurate. It was nice to be able to add my own notations to the maps. I felt like a timber cruiser scouting ahead, or a trapper or fur trader routing trap lines or trade routes. I wondered, did anyone else notice that there was a creek connecting these lakes? There were many smaller creeks that connected lakes and rivers not shown on the map. Many of the spots I found looked like no one had been to them in decades—there were no plastic bottles, no candy wrappers, no discarded worm containers, or shotgun shells either.

There was so much open land waiting to be explored, and I wanted to be the one to do it. There were hunters who returned to the same places year after year, campers with favorite spots, and high-school kids who had favorite places to party where the cops would not be called to break it up; but no one else knew it all, no one else took the privilege to explore it all. There were also so many other areas that were forgotten about. My goal was to be able to look at a map and be able to picture what was there in my mind.

As I would go around bends in the creeks, sometimes I felt as if the deer bounding away held a secret, and I continued on my trips even when I felt too tired to continue. I would be the only living person to know what was around the next bend.

Sitting in my kayak, soaked in sweat, many miles downstream from my starting point made me feel accomplished. I felt that I was exactly where I should be.

CHAPTER 5

It was May. The fully open fishing season was coming around again. I dug around under rocks and stumps to find worms for the fishing opener. I decided to try fishing in the Rice River for my first time out. I tramped over dry brown grass and through stands of leafless trees under a gray, overcast sky. I found an otter swimming where I first stopped, so it seemed that I might have picked a good location. I sat on the bank for about an hour without catching anything. Then snowflakes started to come down.

It was May and it was snowing. Why was it snowing? Why were the fish avoiding my bait? Maybe it was not such a good location. Maybe the otter did not know what it was doing, or was just out enjoying the day and getting some exercise in the process. I wondered how otter tasted as I bit into my peanut butter and blackberry jam sandwich. The sandwich was something to whet my appetite only; I planned on frying up a pan of fish for my next meal.

A few nibbles were all I got after I sat around for another hour. The grass along the river was still brown and dried up, even with open water on the lakes, frost would still be found in many places if I dug down a foot or two. The Swede heads, slang for the clumps of roots and grass that form in marshes and make unsteady stepping stone substitutes, extended along the river as far as I could see. The hardwoods along the river still had not been producing buds, but within a week things would start to look very green everywhere around me. I decided that I still had a lot of time left to go fishing before the lakes and rivers froze over again, and it would not signal the end of the world if I did not catch anything on opening day. I felt like moving around a little more.

Despite growing up on a lake, I never took fishing seriously until after I lived in the Twin Cities. I was twenty-three years old before I ever bought a fishing license. I went out fishing with some of the friends I made at the resort when I was younger, but by the time I turned sixteen I was not interested in fishing. I did not have a lot of gear for fishing; an all-purpose rod and reel for casting, a collapsible rod for backpacking, a fly rod for trout, and when I felt like being a sport with the smallmouth bass, a net, and four plastic snap-cases filled with tackle in a soft-sided tackle bag. When I wanted to hike back to a new fishing spot, I did not have to worry about what I needed to bring with me, I just grabbed my pole and tackle bag, and I had everything with me I needed.

I decided to drive to Little American Falls on the Big Fork River. The land on both sides of the waterfall and campsites there were maintained by Koochiching County, and the sign at the end of the unassuming rutty gravel road adjacent to hayfields insured that no curious parties would just stumble across the scene there. Anyone wishing to visit the waterfall for the first time needed to know the general location of the road and needed to really pay attention to their surroundings as they went in search of it.

The gravel road led to a campground on the northeast side of the Big Fork River. To my right as I turned into the campground, I saw a steep hill leading down to a set of wooden stairs. Depending on the time of year, I might be able to see the river below. To the north of the stairs was a viewing area with a bench that faced down the hill toward the huge chunks of granite and crashing water known as Little American Falls.

The wooden stairs on the hill led down to a flat grassless path, which worked its way toward the falls. The well-trodden dirt path continued along the river and went up and down over the eroded places and the clay and black dirt. There were a few trees, which served as a sort of railing as the path continued along the river. When there had been rain, the slope got very slippery. Always evident were the places where other travelers had slipped and slid down the hill. Cedars lined the hill on the banks along the waterfall, and the trees seemed to hold in moisture. An early memory always projected itself in my mind when I visited the falls, and I imagined a faint mist working up the hill even when there were clear blue skies and sunshine.

The water was rushing over the rocks and spilling out into areas it would not reach during the dry height of summer. I found quite a few people fishing below the falls, and I did not want to be a part of the crowd.

I decided to head back to my camp and read a book. I had heard that the fishing was terrific below the waterfall at certain times of the year, but I'd never had any luck. Of course I always left when the crowds built up, and they were often around for a reason.

As I returned to my camp from Koochiching County, I stopped at a sign for Itasca County. On early maps, Itasca could be seen covering almost all of northeastern Minnesota before being split into Itasca, Koochiching, St. Louis, and Lake counties. The county also lost land to Lake of the Woods, Beltrami, Aitkin, and Carlton counties as settlers started to move in, and the land was being surveyed. The county was named after Lake Itasca, the headwaters of the Mississippi; cutting the first and last three letters from the Latin words *veritas caput*, meaning true head, shortened the name.

The Forest Service sign at the established dispersed campsites stated that there was a fourteen-day limit for camping. I followed the rules and moved my camps before the time limit was up. I was thinking about moving back and forth between my first and second camps for a while because there was still plenty of dead and downed trees for firewood at the first site that I could go back to, and the first camp felt like home after I had spent so many days wandering the forest there and following the deer paths through the woods. The squirrels especially provided entertainment while I was preparing my meals since they would chase after each other and try to steal scraps of food in front of me.

I was watching a pair of squirrels chasing each other around through the tree tops one day when the pursuing squirrel missed a branch and plummeted to the earth. It lay on the ground for a few moments, then started chirping and went scampering up the nearest tree to resume its business.

No matter what I had been doing throughout my life, the days would always fly by once I got into a routine. I had wished to break away from this cycle and make every day something different, but I was now making the same rounds. I thought about it and realized I did not really care—plans change, and I laughed.

CHAPTER
6

T he weather was still very cold, with intermittent drizzle for over a
week. I stopped in one day to see my friend Hal. Hal had chosen to stick
around when everyone else from our class was moving away. His parents
owned a gas station and garage. He had been baptized in motor oil and
never thought twice about what he wanted to do with his life; he was an out-
standing mechanic and probably could have found a job anywhere, but he
wanted to stay put and drive the tow-truck for the family business. We went
to Moonshine Lake to try our luck with the trout. No real luck there. We
set up a camp and shared beer and stories around the fire. The next morning we drove over to Trout Lake and hiked back to the Joyce estate.

Hal had been gambling a lot, drinking a lot, and was still looking
for a girlfriend. There are not many people around, so life could get lonely.
Hal's life was a perfect example of some of the things that could make life
hard in the woods. There were more casinos being built, and for many people who lacked money gambling was a chance to get rich quick. It was also
a way to stay busy for the night. Someone could go to the casino with ten
dollars and play the slot machines all night. There were plenty of people
around, and it was a social atmosphere, one that was not a bar—although
there was plenty of alcohol to be had at the casino.

The Joyce estate was a huge family compound currently being run
by the Forest Service. William Joyce began buying up timber rights and

land around the area in the 1880s. The Joyce property around Trout Lake was logged by the Itasca Lumber Company at the turn of the century. All of the logs were driven along the chain of lakes leading to the Prairie River and the Mississippi. The Itasca Lumber Company had their hands full getting all the logs out of there. The age before roads and trains presented mountains of difficulty for transporting such heavy, bulky items as sixteen-foot sections of log, sometimes four or five feet in diameter.

Looking at the areas where the log drives would have had to take place boggles the mind. Gigantic logs were being rolled and prodded through a few inches of water. Those constructing dams were as dependent on the right weather conditions as farmers, a year with no snow would mean bankruptcy for a company and four or more months of back-breaking labor without reward for the men working to get the trees cut down and ready to be transported to the sawmills.

David Joyce decided to build a retreat out on the Trout Lake property and had a trail built up to an area for a hunting cabin in 1924. Joyce had around thirty buildings constructed to build a family compound. Many of the original structures still survive in good condition, along with some very large white pine that remain on the property and scattered throughout the forest. While wandering through the cabins and around the white pine, I thought to myself that no matter how well the buildings are constructed or how well the lumber was weather-proofed and cared for, the wood was always longer lasting when it stood connected to the roots that nourished it.

Today Trout Lake is a semi-primitive area accessible to hikers, canoeists, and kayakers, with a few historical resort cabins remaining as artifacts of a different age and an imprint of wealth on the earth. There is no real public boat access, only a private one, as well as places a canoe or kayak could be carried through to reach the lake. The short portage to the water is well worth it.

We hiked around the area, and I decided to stay there for the night, while Hal had to leave so he could make it to work.

The next morning I started to feel a fever coming on. I gathered firewood and explored the property as my fever built throughout the day. I kept pulling on more and more layers of clothing and throwing more wood on the fire but the fever kept me shivering. I could have hiked back to my truck, but I was not going to see a doctor or travel to a more hospitable climate, so I figured the estate was as good of a place to convalesce as any.

I grew even sicker the following day. I watched the whitetail deer wandering around the estate and read. I had a sudden strong urge to read one of the books that I left with everything else in my truck, but I was a few miles from my truck and I really did not feel like hiking anywhere.

Entertainment was easy to come by while I was in my weakened state. For a half an hour or longer I stayed enthralled while watching boiling water from my pot disappear into the air as it turned into steam over the fire. I stayed curled up in my sleeping bag for most of the day. There were several squirrels interested in my food supply, especially the bread and crackers. I left a slice of bread out to test the adventurousness of the little varmints, but then I had to fight the little beasts away from my camp for the rest of my stay.

On the third day I started to feel better. I got on my feet and hiked to Doan Lake to see if I could find any sign of a logging camp that was supposed to have existed in the area at the turn of the twentieth century. I found no sign of the logging camp, not that I really expected to, and I briefly wished that I owned a metal detector along with all of the other little gadgets I dragged around with me everywhere I drove.

On the fourth day I was almost back to normal. I had some good reading time while I was laid up aside from the time that I was shivering uncontrollably and was moving onto my third book when I felt good enough to go out for a long hike. On the fifth day at the estate, I was feeling very good and decided that I had spent enough time there.

I found it amazing how quickly the mind and body could forget an illness once it had passed. I felt better than ever. Typically I did not get sick more than once a year, even with just the common cold. I figured I would probably not be sick for the rest of the year since I had made it through my fever. Once I was healthy again, I got in touch with Hal again. He felt bad when I told him about being sick. He said one of his young cousins had been sick before he saw me, and he thought the germs probably came from him.

Hal had a few days off so he could go out exploring and fishing again. Unfortunately every day was not a vacation for the full-time residents of the area. Daily concerns all too often overshadowed the wonders that waited in the out of doors. Hal was the type of fellow who, if ever given the chance, would devote whole weeks to friends and family. The people in the area were some of the most genuine people around.

The area residents formed a working demonstration of how a relatively healthy society should and could work if it were free from crime and fear of strangers and neighbors. I went to the island with Hal after I had fully gotten over the illness. I caught a few bass and took some pictures around Jack-the-Horse Lake. I enjoyed my time greatly. It was a lot different being with Hal when we had no time constraints.

Hal and I ran into a few friends visiting from the Twin Cities for the weekend while we were in Marcell picking up supplies. After getting our supplies, our new guests followed us to our campsite.

We had four more people come out to camp with us—Tom, Jeff, Lisa, and Fudd. I bought a thirty-pack of watered down beer for the camp out. I was set for cheap beer and had a half-liter of whiskey left as well. I did not bring much food across the lake to our campsite because I was hoping to catch enough fish for my meals.

We were camping on a point that I had been working on. I felt uncomfortable having six people there. It was my campsite, after all, at least for the time being. I had dug the fire pit and gathered the wood. I had scouted out the woods around it and found a good place to hang our packs so the bears could not get to them.

Jeff started breaking bottles against the fire ring and then Lisa tossed a bottle too. I yelled at them and told them to have some respect for the place. The group shrugged, and Jeff picked up a few of the biggest shards of glass.

I had known everyone there for years, but I found myself disgusted by their behavior. I felt selfish wanting them to leave, but they were being incredibly disrespectful. I thought of the broken bottles and other garbage left behind, and it made me feel terrible that people I called my friends were making a mess like all the unknown slobs that I had cursed in the past. The camp was my home, but with my home not really belonging to me, I had to wonder where I belonged after witnessing the camp being treated in such a manner. If my friends felt the need to break bottles and litter, I wished they would save it for the city. The next morning everyone but Hal left.

Hal and I went fishing out at Johnson Lake. There was a kid in his early twenties launching his canoe who started telling us everything he knew about the lake and the area. I'm not really sure why he thought we were tourists, but by the end of the conversation we found out that his parents had just bought a summer home, and the two months he had been at the cabin was the first time he had been there. It was nice that someone was so interested in the area.

We drove the forest roads and listened to music for a few hours, then went back out fishing near the island and listened to national public radio and Tom Waits on my portable CD player as we sat by the fire. We shut off the radio several times when the loons out on the lake began getting excited and calling each other.

After breakfast the next day, we went out fishing again. We caught a few very good eating-sized bass. I caught the largest on a new lure that I had splurged on. We went back up on shore, and Hal filleted the fish. I held the flashlight while he got the fish ready for the sizzling pan. We drank our share that night as we talked and sang songs.

The next day we went out to Big and Little Ole Lakes and fished in some very challenging wind. We blew across the lake, paddled back, and repeated the entire process six times. I snagged a plastic bass worm and my line snapped before I could safely give the line more slack and paddle back. Hal lost four lures in the wind and was obviously not happy about it.

We went to the Marcell café the next morning for breakfast. We sat around over coffee and talked to some of the regulars. The cafe served in part as a community center, and it was across the dining room that news and notices were distributed. Impromptu town meetings were held throughout the day, and the cafe seemed to really keep the town running smoothly. After sitting in a canoe for a few days, I like to stretch my legs out a bit.

The snowmobile trail sign at the edge of Marcell got me thinking about all the trails that sat unused for the majority of the year. We decided that we would go out on a few of the trails since we had never heard anyone talk about hiking on them. We would take the next two or three days to hike along some of the snowmobile trails and see what they were like when the forest was green and covered in flowers and weeds.

Hal left his truck at Antler Lake, and the two of us drove up Scenic Highway 7, and over on County Road 45 to 38, 48, and 19 until we found a place to park and unload. We were starting our journey on the Suomi Trail.

There were thousands of popple and birch trees as the Suomi Road curves, rises, and falls over the rolling hills it passes through. At the south end of Grave Lake, the road crosses over a small creek that flows into Little Bowstring Lake and becomes the Bowstring River. The water flows north toward Dora Lake where it becomes the Big Fork River.

Forest Road 2153, also known as the Orange Lake Road, formed the western border of the Suomi Hills recreation area. We drove further up the Suomi Road to the southern border of the Chippewa National Forest. We talked about the horse farms in the area as we stopped at Island Lake.

We turned off onto a series of gravel roads and drove by Cottonwood Lake and to Greenwood Lake. There are many bogs around with creeks interspersed.

The Suomi Trail starts up between the Suomi Road and Highway 38 and winds north through Suomi Hills. The land is hilly, crossed with creeks, and full of marshy moose habitat and stands of pine.

We hiked along the Suomi Trail, up and down the hills, pausing often to take in the sights. The Suomi Snowmobile trail runs to the west of Suomi Hills, and cuts through it where the Orange Lake Road cuts across between Highways 38 and 48. The landscape is very similar to that found on the trails of Suomi Hills—many stand of birch, along with marshy areas and hills. There seem to be many more jack pine along the snowmobile trail. A fox trotted across the trail about fifty yards ahead, it paused and looked back at us lazily along the side of the trail next to the budding ferns. The birch trees grew in tremendously large stands. In places there was a wall of green and white out of the corner of my eye.

A large, beaver-chewed popple tree was ready to fall down next to a creek channel between two lakes. We waded across the channel and ate pistachios by a small fire as we watched the loons fighting against the breeze blowing across the lake. We hiked a few miles back along an old hunting trail. By the time we were back on the main trail, the formerly tottering popple tree had fallen across our path.

That afternoon we were coming through a stand of jack pine up on a hill on the Suomi Trail when Hal stumbled on a loose tree root and banged his shin against a large rock as he twisted and rolled down the hill. He lay there stunned, and I knew from the wince and groan he let out as he tried to stand that he would not be able to finish our hike for a few days. It was probably around forty miles to Hal's truck. If he had hiked even ten more miles with the bang up he had taken, it may have put him out of commission for even longer.

I found a branch for Hal to use a crutch for the next mile until we made it to the Continental Divide and the Bernie Kocian Wayside Rest. We sat at a picnic table at the wayside rest and waited for cars to stop for us to inquire about rides. Past the Continental Divide along Highway 38, all water flows north toward the Hudson Bay.

I always thought of logging when I crossed the Continental Divide. Log drives during the white pine era taking place from the chain of lakes and streams connecting to the Big Fork River led to International Falls and were exported to Canada. Early timber pirates drove the logs into Canada for a profit, heading away from the United States authorities that did not spend much time policing the area anyway. After waiting for about an hour, we were finally able to thumb a ride back up Highway 38 to Highway 19 and my truck.

CHAPTER 7

I awoke to a loud crash outside the nylon walls of my home. At first I thought another branch had come down in the wind, but I decided to investigate anyway. I unzipped the tent and crawled out into the pre-dawn, cold morning in my long underwear. I checked my surroundings and decided the source of my early waking had either been the cardinal sitting on the firewood pile or the very large black bear pawing at my pack, grunting and snorting as it went about its business. My natural instincts coupled with a thorough college education led me to believe it was probably the bear that had awakened me.

I watched as the bear pulled a frying pan out through one of the new openings it had created in the pack and briefly contemplated just crawling back into my sleeping bag for a few more hours and letting the bear have its way.

The bear slowly raised its head from the frying pan it had been licking to look at me. It decided I was no threat and resumed its licking as I fumed and cursed it. I grabbed my rifle and got to my feet, soaking my wool socks with the morning dew as I watched the bear ignore me. I shot into the air several times, which was enough to get the bear to raise its head again. I shot once more, but not until I aimed at the bear did it decide to slowly walk away.

"Go find a summer home to break into. You'll give the yuppies something to talk about when they show up." I yelled after it as it ambled through the willows on the south side of my camp.

I decided I might as well stay up. It was difficult to get up and stay motivated on the cold mornings after a storm. Under normal circumstances on days like this, I might sleep until eight or nine. I got a fire going and threw some grounds into my coffee pot as I contemplated breakfast, finally deciding that a stringer of bass would set the day up just right. I grabbed my fishing pole and walked down to my kayak at the lake. The time of the day was right, and I hoped the next storm I could see rolling in would have the fish biting.

Within an hour I had caught eight decent-sized bass, so I turned back toward camp to beat the storm. I sipped at my coffee as I filleted and fried my catch. I had five slices of bread left. I ate two with my fish and decided to keep three for sandwiches. I was planning to follow the small creek that led out of the lake that afternoon to break up some of the beaver dams blocking it, but the sky didn't look very friendly.

I knew it was my fault the bear had come into camp. I should have put my pan up in a tree like I did with my food, but I'd hiked a long way the day before and by the time I got back I had forgotten the pan was still in the pack. The bears were coming out of hibernation and they were hungry.

I cursed the bear for ruining my pack but told myself the old frame pack creaked too much anyway. I'd sewed and patched it more times than I cared to remember. I had smaller backpacks I could use until I made a trip into town in a month or two. That bear had probably weighed about five hundred pounds, and it certainly could have done a lot worse. When it gained back the weight it had lost in hibernation, it might weigh seven hundred pounds.

When I was younger, we sent guests to an open garbage pit to watch the bears. I spent many nights watching the bears pulling apart piles of garbage at the pit.

The open pit dumps were no longer around, but bears still went for garbage. Occasionally I would come across shredded garbage bags with whatever the bears had not considered edible strewn through the trees.

I thought back to living in the city during college and how someone had broken into my house and stolen my stereo, guitar, and bike, along with a truckload of other things from my roommates and me. Now I was living miles from the nearest house, and I still had to worry about intruders coming and stealing my meager possessions. I said to myself that even if that damn bear had eaten all my food and were to keep coming back for more, I would still prefer bears to humans for neighbors, and I laughed.

CHAPTER
8

I began going out fishing more often as June approached, and I was doing very well. I would filet my catch on shore and toss the cuts in my pan with some batter. I did not have to be at my camp to enjoy a quick meal. There were many days when I ate only fish.

I felt better because I was able to secure my own food and skip going to the supermarket. Since I had no new money coming in, every savings helped. I was that much further removed from the impersonal life I had experienced surrounded by buildings and people in the cities with every bite I took. The lakes in the Twin Cities were stocked with fish, but there were always fishermen taking the fish right back out again. I did not feel like eating anything from the water anywhere near factories, power plants, or even gas stations.

I was staying at the northeastern end of the Chippewa National Forest, and driving the Jingo Lake Road almost daily. The road ran east and west between highways 38 and 6 and was a portal to a wilderness area at the edge of the National Forest land. The gravel road was kept in good condition by the Forest Service, although before the summer tourist season started, fixing sinkholes and removing downed trees was performed a bit slower. There were often trees across the road for a day or two after large storms. I found it best to have a saw along if I planned on getting through after a storm. ATVs were allowed on trails that shot off from the road, with some areas being very muddy after storms. There were no extravagant signs marking the trailheads.

The Ruffed Grouse Society maintained a hunting trail system on the north side of the road. There was also a rock ATV trail running nearly parallel to Highway 6 on the west side. Further north there were old forest roads accessible to hikers and reached by walking through the forest.

There were several small lakes around, and many marshy areas. Mornings often found the air around small ponds painted with fog. Hiking through the fog in the early morning daylight, especially before the rays from the sun really appear in the sky, was like being on another planet. During years with a lot of precipitation it was best to bring rubber boots on any excursion.

In the fall, the stands of maple showed their changing colors, every day the area seemed different. There were stands of jack pine mixed in with the balsam, spruce, white pine, black spruce, and tamarack bogs. Several very large white pines remained in the area, trees that escaped the white pine logging era.

Various creeks wound through the area, sometimes choked with weeds, but early in the spring before things really started to turn green for the summer I could see the channels the beavers had worked through in the floating grass islands. Loggers cut through the area at the turn of the twentieth century, and there were several deadhead logs found on Jingo Lake and the creeks that feed into and out of it. Looking at the land today, I was amazed that any sort of log driving could take place in such shallow water.

When June arrived, there were more people around in the woods. Kids were finishing up their school year, and the family vacations were starting. I went over to a gravel pit along Highway 38 and set up a camp at Burr Lake.

My camp needed a lot of work. I spent a few days there and cleaned the woods out, bringing all of the garbage out near the road and piling it where it could be picked up. There was a lot of garbage dumped out around the fire pit. I found a few old couches, a lawnmower, television sets, and a lot of smaller household garbage. There was also a deer that wolves had torn apart, and hair was spread out under the balsams.

I found three deer hoofs in the balsams to the west of the gravel pit. Under the branches, I came across a deer skull that had only been slightly gnawed on by the porcupines.

Marcell, with a year round population of around two hundred people, was beginning to seem like a sizable bastion of civilization after being on my own for a few months. ASV, which manufactures track trucks, started in the building where the Marcell Family Center is now. There is a sawmill, three restaurants, two hotels, post office, bar, liquor store, three antique shops, a bait shop, gas station, landscaping business, two realty offices, and town hall, although there are about three times as many businesses as buildings.

Marcell was known as Turtle Lake when it was founded in 1905, but, in order to differentiate itself from other towns, the residents changed the name in honor of Andy Marcell, a conductor on the Minneapolis and Rainy River Railroad, which ran through Marcell from Deer River to Craig in Koochiching County. I went through Marcell to pick up fresh bait when I didn't feel like digging around in the dirt or trapping minnows.

I drove to Bigfork to get a few groceries and some ale and saw a flyer for the Bigfork Wilderness Days celebration being held on main-street the following day. There was going to be live music, a parade, and fry bread.

I drove there to check it out and see if I saw anyone I knew. I recognized some of the people in attendance, but none of the friends that I had grown up with were there.

I had gone to school in Grand Rapids and spent most of my time near the far end of Highway 38. I had several friends from Bigfork and Deer River that I was always going to visit. I got to know the roads pretty well from being out with my friends.

I watched the parade and stayed for the street dance. As the attendees got drunker, a few approached and asked who I was. I found out that stories had started to circulate about me from the people I had talked to and seen. No one was sure if I was some new type of hippie, a demented tourist, survivalist, bank robber, or government worker.

I went kayaking on a small tributary of the Rice River the day after the Bigfork Wilderness Days celebration. The creek would pass by my camp, but I tried getting into it at another location and going to my camp on a water route. I hauled my kayak out of the back of my truck into the shallow creek along Highway 38. The route I was trying immediately revealed to me that I would not have an easy trip. I had to portage over quite a few beaver dams to continue up stream.

When I got on top of the largest beaver dam, I got out and pulled my kayak over it. When I stepped back into the kayak, it started to move away from the dam. I had my cooler sitting in the cockpit right where I attempted to put my other foot. I swayed back and forth momentarily and lost balance, plunging into the murky water. My hat came off and was floating next to me when I surfaced. I had not fallen out of my kayak before and felt embarrassed around the birds in the brush that fortunately were my only audience. I was in stinking water, but I felt strangely happy. It was a sweltering day and it felt great to be in the water, even being coated in grime.

I crawled out and sat on top of the beaver dam. Luckily, no water had flooded into the kayak, and I did not lose anything aside from my pride. I stripped down to my underwear and spread my clothes out over the bow and stern of the kayak to dry. With any luck, I would stay upright and would not lose any of the clothes in the water as I continued.

My camp was farther west—I had to press on. I did not want to return to my truck with wet clothes and no new knowledge about the creek. I told myself that I could either keep going in my kayak, or I would have to return to camp a defeated man and put on my waders to walk down the stream and over all of the lumps of grass and hidden holes and bumps to trip me up. I kept paddling upstream. It was sunny out, so my clothing dried quickly. I pushed myself up onto the bank and had lunch.

A beaver swam directly underneath me several times. It was eerie to see beavers moving under the water. The beaver is a very powerful animal and, with glare coming off the water, it can appear as all manner of things to the dangerous combination of the human eye and imagination. With all of its fur compressed to its body and moving along rapidly like an underwater torpedo, the beaver appears as an otherworldly creature. I could imagine early humans attempting to describe the beaver and it being imagined as a monster.

The beaver is a trickster as well. These animal incarnations of Loki move in close, surface and slap their tails very loudly to startle intruders. Many nights when I was drifting calmly with the current, my nose stuck in a book, I found the slap somewhat startling, even if I knew it was coming. As I watched a beaver swimming back and forth underneath me, I thought back to my hat floating in the murky water a few hours previous. Two hundred years ago, I may have imagined that beaver as a hat swimming under the water; it would have been the height of men's fashion.

I moved through some very narrow channels in the creek. There were a few places I worked through not knowing if I would be able to turn around after all of the effort I had expended. Some of the narrow waterways ended up leading to another wider section of the creek, some disappeared suddenly. Each time I reached one of these dead ends, I planted my paddle firmly into the bottom of the creek and stood up to survey the marshy grassland in front of me. In many places, it would have been easier to just get out and pull the kayak. The thought led to Humphrey Bogart pulling leeches off himself in *The African Queen*, after pulling the boat through a swamp.

Often, looking out over the marsh, it was hard to make out where any of the waterways were, or to make out the direction I had just come from. I went to the end of several fingers of the creek that reached out into the marsh. After exploring five long dead end channels, I ran out of options and turned around. I felt as if I had been paddling around in the palm of a giant.

On my way east, I pulled out through a different creek and ended up back at Burr Lake. There were ducks everywhere. I came across a U.S. Forest Service sign designating the Chippewa National Forest in a virtually inaccessible patch of marsh. It seemed more fitting to see the sign there than along the side of a tar highway. I paddled back to my camp to get some dry clothes before I continued along the creek to the beaver dam and the site of my earlier mishap.

CHAPTER
9

I had been spending all my time in the woods finding my own places to hike and explore. As exciting as it was seeing new places everyday and creating my own maps, I felt I needed a bit of time off to relax and see where the tourists went. I decided to visit one of the established parks. I could set out on a trail and know exactly where I was all the time; that would be a very different experience.

As roads and automobiles appeared around Bigfork, the town slowly turned into the sprawling cityscape it is today, a community of well over 400 people. Scenic State Park was an area saved from logging and farming and remained a place to get away from toil and for the home-steaders to visit to remember what the Big Fork Valley was like before they arrived.

The inactive fire tower on the north side of Coon Lake offers an example of how forest fires were spotted and attended to before getting too out of control. Unfortunately the tower was locked. At one time, phone lines were strung up through trees and across creeks and rivers to keep warnings as current as possible about fire conditions and fires in progress around Northern Minnesota. The Scenic State Park tower is the size and style being built in the 1930s in Minnesota by the Civilian Conservation Corps, Minnesota Forest Service, and U.S.F.S. personnel- a 100-foot tower with an eight-by-eight-foot cab.

I next made my way to Pine Lake and had a picnic there. My picnic consisted of chips and soda, power food for hiking. Looking out at the lake, it seemed like it was drizzling at times, but it was only bugs teasing the fish.

The soft needles covering the forest floor around Pine Lake were home for the night. I had a fleece sleeping bag that I rolled out and laid on top of, though covering up was not necessary with how warm the night air stayed. I returned to my truck in the morning so I could get an early morning paddle in. I unloaded my kayak and paddled around Coon and Sandwick lakes. The lakes were fairly quiet until the afternoon, and then families started to show up to launch their boats and lay on the beach. I found an old life jacket, a pair of shorts, and three fishing lures washed up along the shore.

I had always gone camping, and on hikes in the woods, but I did not realize that I actually needed to have these things in my life. I was accustomed to living with nature all around until I got to the Twin Cities, and then I recognized how claustrophobic I felt.

The wind started to pick up when I was on my way back across Sandwick Lake, and I was fairly sweaty by the time I fought my way back to the landing.

I sat pouring over maps, looking farther north to Voyageur's National Park, which I had visited during my vacation. I wanted to feel at home in all of Northeastern Minnesota—the area that was formerly all mapped as part of Itasca County.

I went to Lake of Isles, also a part of Scenic State Park, and read a book until the wind died down in the evening. There was much to explore at Lake of Isles with several back bays, beaver lodges, and hills. The first bay I went into was a circle pond that ran through a marsh on the west end of the lake. Beavers had been using it for hundreds of years. On the east side of the lake were very old, twisted white pines. The pines did not reach skyward, but rather toward the nearby trees, the unfortunate victims of white-pine blister rust. White pines seem to spring out of the ground fully formed; the top and bottom of the tree look very different. When the top comes through, the bark is very smooth and light, as the tree grows the bark changes and becomes dark, rough, and furrowed.

There are mounds sloping fifteen to twenty feet above the water that create miniature islands on the east end. In deeper water are rough-gravel beaches with cedar, spruce, and pine growing on them, surrounded by driftwood hundreds of years old. Highway 7 passes between a bay of the lake and the rest of the park, so the occasional truck rumbled by as I paddled. I found a few snap traps, which are carnivorous plants, back among the lily pads. There were not many around, and I counted myself lucky to see them. I found an inner tube in one of the back bays and hauled it back to the dock as drizzle started to come down.

Hal discovered that he had broken something in his ankle, so he would not be able to join me again for a time. I thought back to the earlier journey we had started. I wanted to keep hiking on the snowmobile trail. We had started referring to our aborted hike on the Suomi Trail as "The Long Walk." I decided I would start out by going hiking on the Marcell snowmobile trail and cover the ground that we had not reached yet. I would hike from Marcell to Effie and back. I had no time limit, and I had enough supplies for a very comfortable week of hiking.

The road was up against water, and a steep hill jutted up on the other side of the road. I looked down from that steep hill at the lake and watched a fisherman untangling his line from nearly everything in his boat in his attempt to catch anything at all. The hike would be a good change of pace from all of the kayaking I had been doing for the last few weeks. I parked my truck along a forest road as the sky was starting to lighten up for the coming day, then connected with the Marcell Trail and began my new "Long Walk." I first hiked between Butterfinger and Northome lakes. The loons were very vocal as I watched them fishing that morning.

I hiked up on the steep hill overlooking Highway 38 and North Star Lake. There was a warming house, picnic table, and fire pit with griddle up at the top of the bluff. The view to the east revealed a cedar swamp sloping downward and beyond part of the same glacial deposit of sandy soil that had been used for over eighty years by locals around Marcell for road building. There were many rolling, sand hills covered in the green and white of paper birch trees. The sand helped to construct Highway 38. The sand also is supporting large stands of popple, birch, and willow.

A breeze was blowing at the top of the hill, and I sat on a rotten bridge and watched the cars as they passed—one or two every fifteen minutes or so. I wondered where all of these people were going.

I had to think about it for a few minutes to figure out what day it was. I kept a journal, but it was sometimes weeks between when I would get back to recording my thoughts in it.

I encountered plenty of deer and other wildlife along my way. The only things yet to appear were the flowers, plants, and fungi of summer, assuming that former patterns were followed and that year did not bear witness to a season being skipped entirely, which happened occasionally. The grass had not grown up too high yet, so it was very easy hiking. I knew that every tree and every bit of the forest I was walking through would look a lot different as the season progressed.

There were a lot of wood ticks out. I stopped counting how many I pulled off of myself at fifty, I could better use my faculties. I did not always bother pulling the ticks off my clothing right away, and I would have wasted a lot of time if I had bent over every time one got on my boot. I was walking up and down over hills and crawling over and under blown-down trees. There were deep ruts and mudholes in the low areas with springs. The trail was also used by four-wheelers in many places, though none had been through recently, but past use had killed the grass, so I had a clear path to walk. Several trees down over the trail had been cut up into firewood-sized chunks. If it had been a little later in the day, I would have been tempted to set up a camp along the trail. Traveling on foot is the surest and safest way to get anywhere, although if time is a factor it can present other problems. The trail was very muddy in spots, and I had to stop to scrape clods of dirt off my boots.

There were creepy, crawly things out all along the trail. Frogs swam in the four-wheeler ruts and painted turtles sat in the sun with the garter snakes. As I passed by a beaver pond, the grass next to me started to sway. I went to investigate and saw a snapping turtle with a shell about a foot and a half in diameter. I followed it through the grass to see where it would go until it slid into the water of the pond.

I spotted a little doll alongside the trail. I stopped to pick up the doll and saw that it was a bunny with a hard plastic human face. It was kind of a strange toy, and I found the face on the doll a bit sinister, but I decided to hold onto it anyway. I camped out at Snow Lake, putting the creepy token of my journey up in a tree to ward off spirits. I hiked around the Northeast side and saw five pairs of wood ducks out on the lake.

The morning air was completely quiet and still as I looked out over Snow Lake, and then a bass leapt out of the water. The sound of the bass leaping was like an explosion next to the occasional crackling of my morning campfire. I caught a few bass casting from shore. There were not many channels clear of lily pads, but I found one, and the fish seemed relentless. Cast after cast I pulled in fish. I had never had much luck fishing for bass from the shore, so this was quite the surprise.

At Logging Sleigh Lake, I took out my harmonica and buzzed out a couple of fast tunes. The mosquitoes were coming out, and there seemed to be more of them by the minute. I continued on my way through Bigfork, although I stopped to buy some fresh fruit and peanuts.

The Effie Cafe still had lights on when I hiked into Effie, so I sauntered in nonchalantly to get supper. There were a few lingering glances at my muddy clothing and huge frame backpack, but no sign of alarm. I had been hiking through the mud in the woods for nearly two days. After my supper I crossed Highway 5 and found a place to set up camp for the night. I planned to hike to Craigville and the Big Fork River next to it the following day.

The morning dew was soaking me up to my knees on a backwoods deer trail. I thought about all the places I used to have to be at this time of the day. Schools and jobs had always demanded my attention, always coming during the best hours of the day. I had bounced around in a lot of jobs, and no matter what I had been doing, I always wanted to be outside. One of my favorite jobs had been mowing lawns. Unfortunately so many people were looking for work in landscaping that competition was high. I could have been happy working for a lot longer if I had been able to stay with a lawn-care company.

The hike had been going by too quickly, and I was surprised that I could still get out of bed with just minimal soreness in the mornings. I felt great. I was enjoying the sights and the quiet of the morning. I reached the top of a grassy, sparsely treed hill as the sun started showing. The land was different. There were fewer trees, more bushes, and more grass. Minnesota slowly turned into bogs further north, but there was evidence of them along the whole trail.

A yellow-bellied sapsucker woodpecker was working hard on a popple snag off the trail. I followed it and noticed a few old brown bricks in the grass. I circled around and uncovered the corner of an old foundation. I had found the remnants of an old homestead back off the trail. I wandered around prodding at suspicious looking mounds with my walking stick to see what was hidden under the grass and moss. I found what looked to be an old silo foundation, as well as a house. There were some old cast-iron stove pieces and a rusted bed frame among the bricks. The property continued down a hill to a small pond. A few hundred yards from the edge of the pond I located two holes that looked to be about the size of humans, and I wondered if there were people that were buried there at one time. I was near Craigville, after all.

Craigville, now a ghost town, had been very rough and tumble when it was around. It had sprung up to service the lumberjacks who came out to earn a wage in the Northwoods of Minnesota during and after the white-pine logging era and came away with a strong-enough reputation to keep any sign of organized law enforcement miles away at all times. The story of Craigville was similar to other boomtowns across the country. Seemingly overnight new tarpaper shacks had appeared which housed hundreds of bottles of blinding whiskey and women sold into servitude by unconcerned fathers, uncles, and brothers.

The population of Craigville had been a mix of prospectors and lumberjacks, along with the operators of the gaming houses, saloons, brothels, and laundries that came to service the dirty, lousy throngs of lonely men. There was nothing that could be considered respectable in polite circles at that time about the town. Craigville was as tough as they come. Bodies that occasionally surfaced and could be found floating in the river showed that. At the time of the town, entrepreneurs even built their establishments on stilts over the river and installed trap doors in the floors of their buildings for easy, anonymous disposal of bodies.

The women were seldom beautiful or young, but, after working out in the woods without the company of women for four or five months, pretty much anything with a pulse would do.

The buildings with wooden floors showed the scars of the men's calked boots—and they gave the casual observer a glimpse of what the scourge known as "logger's smallpox" would look like on the face and chest of any man who lost his balance and fell to the floor in a fight.

When I got to Craigville I saw nothing but a clearing along the river. I walked around the former site of Craigville. This had been the source of many local legends. Kids growing up in the area could claim bragging rights when they would tell stories of their great-grandfather or grandpa in the logging camps and blowing out their stakes in Craigville. The life that the men lived was one of aging anonymity in the face of history. The lives of the early loggers created a way for those who had grown up in the area a link to the past remained.

My hike back went by quickly. I was showered on a few times, but I stayed dry enough without having to change my clothing. The wind was picking up when I got near Jack the Horse Lake, and I saw a large spruce swaying dramatically in the wind. I sat down, opened a book, and watched the spruce out of the corner of my eye. The forest floor was covered in fallen trees; it was exciting to know that the spruce would soon be joining the other debris. I sat near the tree for a little over two hours, the creaking of the trunk growing louder and louder, until finally it started moving south and groaned as it continued to topple. The roots ripped out of the ground, and the tree fell into a fifty-foot tall popple tree nearby, and snagged for a moment, as time seemed to stop. The tree slowly twisted until the top of the popple splintered, cracked, and continued the descent to an earth-shaking finale. It was a remarkably peaceful ending for such a large tree. I decided to camp next to the shattered stump that night.

The next morning I went fishing, picturing the huge tree crashing down the whole time, and caught breakfast. After eating I went out exploring and found a different spruce with perfect branches for climbing. As I climbed the tree, I imagined it had been seeded at the same time as the one that had fallen the night before. I brought some peanuts up the tree with me and looked down at Caribou Lake as I sat perched near the top of the tree eating nuts like a squirrel.

CHAPTER
10

T here was a secret lake with several islands on it where I had been camping at since I was five years old. The particular island that I had first
gone to with my dad and one of his friends when I went there the first time
was always my island of choice. The lake was not easy to get to, and the
island did not show signs of humans presence that could be found on care-
ful examination at other backwoods campsites. At most campsites the leav-
ings of other people could be fairly assessed by digging through the duff
and finding the small things left behind, such as bottle caps and steak bones.
Often odd nails and hooks could be found among trees near campfire rings.
Camping and fishing at that secret lake was one of the oldest memories I
had.

A grown-over trail circled about three-quarters of the lake and
there were many great places to set up camp and plenty of firewood. The
red pine grew large in the area and provided shelter from the rain. There
were always largemouth bass of a good size for eating to be caught in the
lake, and there were loons that would return year after year. The best part
of the lake was the island though. Toward the west end of the lake there
was a small island that was a great place to camp. I had been back to it many
times over the years with friends and alone. Even though there were signs
of other people having camped or fished at the lake, I could usually show up
and have it to myself at any time.

For three days I camped out on the island fishing, swimming, and lounging in my hammock. It had sprinkled off and on while I was there, but drizzle during the warmest part of the year was more refreshing than an annoyance. One evening I heard a vehicle bouncing along the heavily rutted dirt road that was the only route to the lake. I saw a truck pull up across the lake where my truck was parked and heard two doors slam.

A man and woman walk to the shore, and then I began hearing my name called—"Cole, Cole, it's Ed." I pulled out my binoculars and recognized the man as being my friend Ed. I was not sure who the young woman with him was, but I hollered back to them that I was alone and to come out. They unloaded a canoe and a few other things and within ten minutes were pulling up to the island.

"I'd recognize that beat-up truck anywhere. You probably haven't washed it since the last time I saw you." Ed had a considerable beard that was new since I'd seen him last, but the way he carried himself would give him away no matter how different he looked.

"It's still holding together. Good to see you, Ed. Who's your friend?"

"This is Karen, I found her in a coffee shop in Superior."

"Nice to meet you. Ed has told me a lot about you," Karen said. She was short and skinny with long brown hair that reached her waist.

"Well, that's nice of you to say . . . yeah, we've known each other a long time."

Karen jumped in, "Seriously, I have heard a lot of stories."

I started running through a list in my mind of stories that she could have heard about me. Okay, so maybe there were a lot of them.

"Well that's good. I guess you don't have to ask too much about me then. Of course I don't know anything about you."

"I'll get the cooler and you can hear all about her," Ed said as he grabbed a battered green cooler I recognized instantly. The cooler had been around since our high school party days, and had been along on many expeditions since then.

We walked up to my fire, and he pulled out beers and brats for us all. I threw a few more logs on the fire, and we started cooking. We mixed black and tans while we watched our food sizzling. Karen had grown up in Superior and had been playing at the same coffee shop that Ed had shown up at for years. Ed arrived after she had already played her songs, and she introduced herself when he finished.

They had gone for a walk along Lake Superior that night and hit it off well. They had been together two months, which was a new record for Ed, and apparently for Karen as well. Ed was living in Duluth, and he had brought Karen back with him to meet his parents and to show her some of the places he liked to visit when he was back in the forest. He had been working at a gas station and taking classes at UMD part time. The gas station had recently been robbed, at gunpoint, fifteen minutes after Ed had left for the night. He swore it was not he.

Karen liked to fish, a lot, so the three of us went out in the canoe the next day and caught lunch. It became apparent after a few hours that she liked fishing even more than Ed or I. We kept hinting we wanted to go for a hike, but she wanted to stay out on the water. I went along with them to Turtle Lake, and we fished there for a few hours before moving to Maple Lake. The road out to the lake had been widened, but no new gravel had been put down, so we bounced against each other as we looked out the window at fresh stumps and skidder tracks. We did not have much luck until around eight o'clock that evening, and then we caught a few walleye. They shared my camp again that night, and we all took turns playing songs and telling stories until it started to get light out again. Through our prodding we got Karen to agree on hiking with us before we fished again.

We went to Suomi Hills the next day. I loaded my kayak in the back of Ed's truck with his canoe. We went out on a morning hike, and then unloaded our watercraft, although we left our fishing poles in the truck so we would not be tempted to break our paddling up too much. We toured the lake and all of the fingers of it and stopped on shore for supper. Karen had a job interview back in Superior early the next morning, so they left and I snuck out and did a little more fishing before I moved on.

Lauchoh Lake stuck out on my map. It was easily accessible and surrounded by marshes and creeks. I needed to see where I could get by navigating the creeks. A creek flowed through Lauchoh Lake and under the Farm Camp Road and into the Rice River on the west end. I decided that I would explore the creek to see if I could find any more Rice River routes. It had been a dry month, and the creek, which, on the map went through to the Rice River was blocked off. There was too much brush and several logs in the way. In the sweltering afternoon heat, I did not want to start sawing the logs out of the way, it would have been too miserable sweating and burning in the hot sun. I launched off of the Farm Camp road after parking my truck as far off the road as I could manage. The road was fairly narrow and some large logging trucks barreled along the gravel back-roads.

Several small creeks blocked with beaver dams split off from the lake. I crossed over the dams with quite a bit of effort, and reached several small ponds. I tried to fish, but I kept getting snagged on roots and sticks the beavers had stockpiled. I was soaked in sweat and mud from portaging over beaver dams, and I had gotten my lunch bag pretty wet splashing water in with my paddle in the backed up bays the beavers had created. My sandwiches looked like a muddy sponge. I got a little grumpy at that point, but they still tasted fine.

There were days when I wondered why I was doing the things I did, but I never regretted it. I always had someplace to go and walk off my frustrations. I did not have the excuse of being stuck someplace that I did not want to be no matter how uncomfortable I got.

CHAPTER
11

T he Camp Five Road ran through an area that still showed signs of the early heavy logging era. The former camp that gave the road its name had been somewhere nearby. Many of the roads, as well as the railroads, were a direct result of the logging companies coming through Minnesota as they scrambled to collect the profits of the last white pine logging state. There were several stands of red pine along the road and a lot of sandy soil that was perfect for pine. On Trestle Lake there remained standing a long path of trestles from a branch off of the Turtle Lake Spur of the Gut and Liver Railroad Line. Logging operations set tracks down temporarily where they needed to move a lot of timber out and then move on to the next area. The west end of the lake hid several rotted out deadhead logs among the bow rushes. The trestles from the Turtle Lake branch of the Gut and Liver Line ran parallel to County Road 14 and then turn east along the Camp Five Road.

Holland Lake was a stop along the water route of Fletcher Creek, which connected with the Big Fork River. I kayaked around the lake on my way to the Big Fork River but was forced back to my truck by a violent thunderstorm. I changed into dry clothes and took a nap in the cab. When I woke up it was still raining. I fried up some potatoes and watched the ducks swimming around by Arrowhead Lake. After the rain passed, I drove down an old logging road to get to a lake a few miles back, but with the rain many portions of the road were too muddy to risk passing through in my truck. I got out and went for a hike. After a few miles, it started to drizzle again and then another downpour started. I was completely soaked through, again. I changed into dry clothes back at my camp and decided to stay there until the skies turned blue and cloudless again.

I got into my kayak at Fletcher Creek and explored around the railroad trestles crossing the creek. I found an old deadhead log that must have been at least four feet in diameter at one time, although the bark was all gone. This log must have been too large to make it through the water routes, and, before the trains came in, there was no kind of power aside from that of beast and man. It was a shame that such a large tree was cut down and was in the end too large to use. Such a large tree, if it had remained standing to this day, would be a very impressive monument. Instead it sat along the shore of a rarely visited lake as a rotting home for snails and dragonflies. Timber lost value if they sat too long, something remaining from even the year before was probably not worth anywhere near the original value.

I scared up several deer along the banks, including an eight-point buck. I could not get through on Fletcher Creek, so I made my way back to my camp.

I felt that I needed to keep exploring the rivers and creeks around the area, but I also wanted to go on a river where I wouldn't have to portage every one-hundred feet or so and where I wouldn't have to keep cutting blown-down trees out of my way. It was a very tiring process when to break trail all the time.

The Farm Camp Road Bridge was my next stop. I launched my kayak on the Rice River and floated upstream toward Bigfork. The joke was on me when I started to encounter shallow spots and blow-downs along the river too. I encountered several trees down over the river that I had to cut away with my bow saw so I could continue on my way.

I found the remains of several wing dams from the logging era. Wing dams were built at shallow places in the river to raise the water level enough for the big "blue butt" logs to pass through. White pine timber is very buoyant, but if the logs were very large they would float quite low in the water. The white pine lumberjacks cut down before the logging trucks and skidder era floated higher in the water than the red pine they began to cut in later years, but the bottom section of the logs were still too big to be maneuvered through the shallow water routes present.

Many log drives had taken place on the Rice River and the Bigfork River, both of them flowing north toward Canada. Trees and the compass direction north were indelibly linked in my mind. I thought it was amusing that the logs from the Chippewa National Forest were floated up to Canada. Did they not have enough trees up there already?

As I drifted down the river, I pondered the events leading up to my being where I was at that time and place. I had been influenced by the Northwoods and had an urge to live alone in the wilderness. I always viewed living in the woods as being part of a bygone era. What really got me thinking was that I could do it on my own, go out and live where I wanted to live without a set schedule or a date book filled with places to be. I had been seeing people living out of their vehicles all over the country while I had been on family vacations. The people I saw seemed to be living where they wanted. I always wondered if I would be able to do it too.

I saw people living out of their vehicles on the beaches in California and Florida, although they did not have to worry about freezing to death. The people living on the beaches seemed dependent on others though. I saw too many beach bums out asking for money from tourists and eating food out of dumpsters. I respected the bums who had special skills like juggling or tightrope walking, but it seemed demeaning that they had to put themselves on display to have money thrown into a hat. I did not think it was glamorous living on the fringes of cities and making due with table scraps. I thought it seemed noble in other situations though. What really got me thinking about getting away from everything seriously was being out in Colorado with my parents one year and seeing a couple parked at a wayside rest in their Volkswagen bus camper.

The couple staying in the camper intrigued me. I watched them while they sat and watched the river. The man had a guitar and the woman beat on a set of bongo drums. They made up songs while their laundry dried. They did not look dirty, and they obviously cleaned their clothing. They seemed to do everything with class as I sat and daydreamed about one day living just like they did.

After we got back to Minnesota, we stopped in at an old Volkswagen dealership that had a wide selection of buses. They had campers, and the normal variety. We got out and I went and looked at the vehicles. I was surprised that only two of the buses were locked. I got to look through models from nearly every year and my imagination ran wild as I made my way through the lot. I wanted to get one of the camper vans for my first vehicle, but my dad told me I would freeze in the winters and if I got into an accident with it I'd probably lose my legs since there was nothing in the front except metal.

As I got older, I never really adapted to the sort of plans that kids from the city had. Growing up in the woods, with such a wide variety of people and differing views, I could not adjust to city life, and I never wanted the things that the city kids wanted.

It never made sense to me to have more with me than I could carry on my own. My house burned down when I was very young and I had two other classmates lose their homes due to fires. I remember one day in class we had firemen come in to explain "stop, drop, and roll" and other fire safety to us.

The firemen said that if a fire broke out, we would not have time to search around for our favorite book or toy; we would have to just leave. I think that statement, coupled with the fire that had already had such a large affect on my life made a lasting impression on me. After that day, I always wanted to keep my things with me. In my classes in grade school I was the first kid to start keeping my backpack and jacket at my desk. I wanted to have it in case we suddenly had to flee the building.

I had been living in the woods for two months, and I really did not feel as if I was missing anything. I no longer missed having running water, and a few tarps strung up in the trees were plenty of shelter from the rain when it came and stored water for me that I did not later have to carry to camp in a bucket. The rain would sometimes drip down through the tarps, but I would just patch the area when the storm cleared and it would be fine until the next hole appeared. I did not miss having four walls. I did not miss having an electricity bill every month. I still got my entertainment fix in with my CD player, and my portable DVD player.

Now that I was living out of my truck, I did not feel as if I was lacking anything. I did not need a permanent address. I had plenty to do without having to worry about a job.

I named my camp after the long lost logging camp I had been searching for. The woods there had once kept a crew of hearty lumberjacks in good health as they supplied timber for the nation. Life had changed a lot. Life was comfortable, and necessities were fairly cheap and easy to come by. I was thankful that I lived in an age when I could experience the things I did as a tourist. I was not required to work daylight to darkness seven days a week, I had enough technology to make life easy and I was allowed to live each day in the way I chose. If things got bad wherever I was, I could always hop in my truck and go someplace else.

CHAPTER 12

O n the first day of July, I went to the Effie café and got a burger and fries. Afterward I drove north on Highway 5 to the nearest bridge crossing the Big Fork River and unloaded my kayak. It was a beautiful day out. Two ospreys circled over the river. I stopped on the banks and walked up to the former site of Craigville. Craigville had changed somehow in the few weeks since I had last been there. As I walked around the banks of the river, I felt as if I was home. I was feeling like I was home more often and in more places now. I quickly grew comfortable with the spots where I set up camp and realized I had similar feelings whenever I passed the places I had stayed or at least spent a considerable amount of time.

The Gut and Liver Line, also known as the Minneapolis and Rainy River Railroad, had spanned from Deer River to Craigville at one time. The Gut and Liver was the logging railroad that was ultimately responsible for humans joining the wolf and moose populations in the area as year-round residents.

I floated downstream to Little American Falls and stopped at the portage for a picnic. I watched the banks of the river closely for any signs of the log drives. The river was loaded with deadheads in this section. So many logs did not make it over the falls. They remained churning in the depths for generations after the last major drives. I wondered how often the logs eventually ended up wherever they were going; some of the logs seemed to be making slow progress. How many of the logs would eventually reach the Rainy River, and how long would it take? No one was around at the falls, so I took the opportunity to do a little fishing there.

I returned to the refuge of the Chippewa National Forest to retrace the route of the Gut and Liver Line. I had a bit of a history refresher as I was picking out my new camp. The place I chose had the grade from the Gut and Liver Line still evident through my new front yard. The railroad grade was still fairly easy to follow through the woods although I had to walk off the grade several times where the brush was exceedingly thick. A little digging along the grade quickly yielded a collection of railroad spikes.

I came across an old dump along the grade that I started excavating with my spade shovel. It was amazing how much was hidden just a few inches under the surface. I found old phonograph players, cast-iron stoves, cans, pans, antlers, boots, tricycles, suitcases, bottles, horseshoes, automobile parts, and toys. It was a mixture of dumpster diving and archaeology going through all of the discards.

There was a stopping place nearby, and I was sure that the loggers and homesteaders riding the train would dump their refuse there. The travelers on the train probably contributed as much to the garbage piles as the railroad workers. I figured there was probably garbage along the entirety of the railroad grade. Many items were still in good condition. I figured I could clean them up and sell them as antiques. I wondered if there were such plentiful dumps along the other railroad grades that rapidly popped up around the state to haul timber to the mills. Archaeologists should not have much trouble putting together some kind of study about the way the early pioneers of the Big Fork River Valley lived and what they had available to them.

A pack of wolves lived near the Gut and Liver camp and kept me company at night. I heard them at night sometimes, and I noticed wolf tracks as I took strolls around the area.

I liked to get a feel for the lay of the land around my camps. I set the boundaries for my camps based on the landmarks. I created maps of my camps with my arbitrary boundaries and visited the edges of the camps every day to make sure no trees had toppled or animals had visited. I knew when I was at the Gut and Liver camp that, if I walked to the black spruce bog on the southeast side, I did not have to walk any further. On the northeast side, the Rice River was the edge of my site. The northwest border was marked by a huge white pine that had been the victim of white pine blister rust and was missing its top. It was a very stocky tree and served as not only a boundary, but a good resting place and reading area as well. Finally, the southwest side was demarcated by a creek that was dry every time I saw it. My boundary lines were by no means straight, but the four reference points gave me a good section of land to explore every day.

In the late nineteenth and early twentieth centuries, loggers and homesteaders moved into Northeastern Minnesota to convert the forest into farmland. In the name of progress, much of the forest was clear-cut and burned over. Crops were planted and livestock like sheep, cattle, pigs, and chickens were brought in.

The timber wolves and other large predators like mountain lions and bears were poisoned, snared, and shot to make the land safe for sheep. There was a bounty paid out by the government for dead wolves, so hunters and trappers could still make a living off wolves when the other animals began to disappear.

But the farms failed, and settlers moved on to more hospitable areas of the country. The land began to turn back into forest, but it was a different kind of forest. White pine could not regenerate with the deer and squirrel populations exploding and eating all the seeds, so fast growing trees like aspen and various brush species began to take over. The new forest was unsuitable for moose, wolves, and the other original inhabitants, but a perfect breeding ground for more deer and squirrels.

At the same time homesteaders and the new inhabitants began to realize the soil and growing season were really not good for farming, the climate delivered the convincing blow, with the snow piling up and the temperature staying below zero for weeks at a time, coupled with the remaining wolves finally convinced many that livestock were not the wisest way to make a living in the woods. Many left because they could not make a living.

Unemployment was around seventy percent in this area during the Depression, so there were many eager to take any work they could get. Massive tree planting and land reclamation efforts were undertaken during the Great Depression, and CCC camps sprang up to alleviate unemployment and disenchantment with the federal government.

The resort and tourism industry began to take off as cities in the Midwest grew exponentially, and people living in them wanted to get away from each other. Deer hunters took over for the wolves in trying to control the deer, and the deer population decreased enough to give more evergreens a chance to grow.

With efforts to return the land more closely to its old image and changing environmental attitudes, wolves very slowly started to return. Wolves are still a rarity, but their population is increasing. They kept themselves hidden well, but I had seen signs of them since I had first moved to the woods. I had never been near a wolves' den, at least not one that I was aware of. One night I heard four or five wolves yelping and growling less than a hundred yards from where I sat.

There is a lot of the wolves' extended family in the area that I had been seeing. There are more coyotes that had been slowly moving into the area. This had never been part of their natural range. It seems that if you drive around after dark you are guaranteed to see a fox, another relative of the timber wolf.

The most common wolf relative in the area is the domesticated dog, and they present the most danger to any explorer of the region. When you see a sign that says "Dogs will bite," or "Beware of dog" it should generally be taken quite seriously.

While staying at the Gut and Liver Camp, I headed northeast to the Smallpox Road. A logging camp in the area had been severely afflicted with smallpox during the winter of 1883. A mass grave remains at the spot. Chief Busticogan, the namesake of several lakes, areas of interest, and menu items at local restaurants, came across the camp on his travels and did his best to help the afflicted, but he was unable to save any of the infected.

The Small Pox Road was mostly just cleared and flattened land. It was more of a glorified trail than a road. It wound through the popple and hardwoods that took over once the pine were logged out. The logging roads were corduroyed in the swampy places. To corduroy a road, trees were cut down, the branches were removed, and then the logs are laid out on the ground side by side like a makeshift bridge. No gravel brought in to improve the road, and after rain it could be very muddy. In a few places after a heavy rainfall I could probably float my kayak through the ruts.

Caldwell Brook meanders through the area. I took my kayak out in it, but it was badly choked with blown-down trees and roots from the eroded banks. I fought and swallowed flies as I worked against all of the snags and the trees that swept across the water. The brook was amazing in that logs had been driven down it at all. I paddled for a few miles and decided to pull my kayak out. I knew that I could make a lot better progress if I just walked along the creek bottom.

The series of logging roads northeast of Highway 1 and Highway 5 extended for miles as the Smallpox Road met with the Gemmell Ridge Road and headed through land that was still logged to this day, although it was done in a much different manner than in the early logging days.

CHAPTER
13

At the Effie Café one morning, I was invited into a conversation by two men in their sixties who had lived in the area their whole lives. One of the men was known only as Santa. The other was Knut. They were discussing trap lines when I first started talking to them. They knew I went out kayaking a lot, and I found out that I had paddled right by Knut one day as he was out scouting new locations. They each made a large portion of their income from selling pelts. The topic switched to horses, and I discovered that Knut was also a horse-trainer, farrier, and horse-logger. I started to ask him more about it, but we were interrupted when our waitress hollered out that his wife was on the phone. Santa and I kept talking while Knut quietly picked up the tab for the table and excused himself back to the ranch.

I stuck around and talked with Santa over coffee. Santa seemed knowledgeable about nearly every subject. I was amazed that he had done so much. Out of all of his interests, I found out that his favorite thing to do was work at his forge blacksmithing. He was the first blacksmith I had met, and I was thrilled. I'd had an interest in blacksmithing since I was very young and spent great portions of my days carving swords and knives out of branches. Blacksmithing is an ancient art—some may argue it's silly to learn in this day and age and would throw around words like "archaic"—but I'd say it's a valuable skill to possess even in the boardroom or office. We talked about blacksmithing, and he said I could stop in anytime I'd like to use his forge. I told him I would like to start right away if it was okay with him. Within a matter of hours, I started to learn the art of blacksmithing.

I was still very far from being able to fashion a suit of armor.

Santa, of course, was the man responsible for teaching the elves of the North Pole the fine art of smiting the black metals, and consequently bringing joy to millions of children throughout the ages as they found quality elven-forged goods under their Christmas trees. As we began working together, he started referring to me as "the wood elf." It was an honor to work with Santa.

I watched him make nails and hooks, and then he showed me how to do some repair work and weld. After my quick lesson, I went to work on my own. He pointed me to a small mountain of iron pieces in the back of one of his sheds. That combined with the pieces I had pulled out of the ground from the Gut and Liver camp, I had plenty of scrap iron around to practice on.

For ten hours on my first day I worked at smiting, taking only a few short breaks while I worked. The hardest part of it all was keeping the forge going. Birch bark provided a steady, hot flame as coke was added to get steady heat. Once the coke was burning, coal was added to keep the forge going. The impurities burned off the coal and left coke, which keeps the fire burning very hot. In order to use the coke, it had to be created first, so a steady rotation had to occur within the forge.

As I went back to visit and use the forge, I learned to draw out and punch metals. I also learned welding. I grew proficient at fixing chains and nails, and I made an assortment of hooks and fasteners. I got a little artistic as well, creating iron doves and moose. I only got burned a few times, and I managed to avoid setting my clothes on fire, dropping the anvil on my foot, or smashing my fingers with the hammer, so all in all it was a safe experience.

Santa was interested in my lifestyle, although, aside from owning property, I did not see the way he was living as being much different from my own. He told me to come back any time.

One of the times I stopped in, he was getting ready to tear down an old garage on his property. He was planning on demolishing it with a backhoe and then burning the unsalvageable wood. I convinced him to let me help, and when he saw the excitement on my face, he told me to hop on the backhoe to knock it over. Most of the boards from the garage had dry rot, and the bottom of the floor had been growing what looked like a tropical rainforest with fungus and mold.

The boards were not usable for any finishing projects, but they would suit my purposes just fine. I used some of the salvaged wood and nails I had fashioned from scrap iron from it to build a tree fort. The scraps made good kindling for my nightly fires. My new tree fort had two tiers to climb around on. I decorated the fort inside and out with some of my new-found antiques.

I typically left my small projects behind for future explorers. I built up rock walls and piled extra firewood. I dug irrigation trenches and moved trees to sunnier areas where they would grow faster. I felt that I owed the forest for letting me stay in it all those months.

As I stayed around the Effie Café throughout July, I got to know the locals. The town was excited about the upcoming rodeo, and I was getting excited for it too. The North Star Stampede was an annual rodeo hosted north of Effie on Highway 5. Howard Pitzen had held the competition at his North Star Ranch for over fifty years, and it seemed to grow in popularity every year.

The rodeo was a three-day affair that always took place during the last full weekend of July. There was free camping on Howard Pitzen's land, and it drew a dedicated crowd year after year from all over the United States and Canada who came to watch the rodeo and party the whole weekend. It coincided with the city festivities of Effie, which included sidewalk sales, live music, dances, bingo, and a parade.

I went to the North Star Stampede on the opening night. The stands were packed and the beer was freely flowing.

The events at the North Star Stampede were bareback bronc riding, calf roping, saddle bronc riding, steer wrestling, team roping, bull riding, and barrel racing. Bull riding, the major event, was divided into two sections. The first section got the crowd cheering, and the second section marked the end of the competition for the night. I talked to some of the riders to find out more about how the rodeo worked.

Each rider paid an entry fee to be allowed to ride in the rodeo and they paid for every event that they entered. The money for each event was taken and the rodeo committee put in extra, which was called "added money" that went to the winner of the event. A rider had to win in order to get money in the rodeo world, so many in the rodeos would travel for thousands of miles from their homes and go home less a considerable amount of money.

The riding competitions were the biggest draw, and the eight seconds the riders had to stay on their animals to qualify was often unmet. The rodeo clowns were in charge of keeping the riders as safe as could be, but there is an ambulance nearby for good reason.

There was a traffic jam as people worked their vehicles back onto Highway 5 from the ranch so I walked back to the camping area to see what sort of drunken shenanigans were occurring. I decided not to stick around at the campground for very long after the competitions ended; there were too many people around and it was too loud for me. I drove back to the Effie Café and ran into Knut outside. He asked me if I would like to ride along with him during the Effie Parade the next night. His grandchildren had decorated the wagon for the parade. Nearly every square inch of the wagon was decorated with horses of every possible type, including some with horns, antlers, or wings.

Effie was very busy when I arrived to meet the wagon the next night. I drove past Knut and found the nearest place to park I could, which was next to Knut's horse trailer on a nice flat area in the ditch on the west side of town. Knut and his wife, Susie, were waiting at the parade staging area with a whole wagonload of little kids that I found out were all of their grandchildren.

Knut brought a team of Percheron draft horses named Henry and Charles to take part in the parade. They were a very beautiful team, snow white and around 1,500 pounds apiece. The team was Knut's finest. They were the horses he used most often when he had a logging job to do. Knut dropped the trees and cut them up. The horses were harnessed, and chains were connected for the logs to be dragged out of the woods. He got a lot of business from summer cabin owners who wanted to thin out the trees on their land while avoiding the damage that skidders and timber processors generally left behind.

There were hundreds of horses walking up and down Highway 1 with their riders. The road was quickly filling up with used hay.

My offer to help got me a stack of flyers for Knut's all-purpose horse business to distribute during the parade. I ended up talking to so many people about Henry and Charles and passing out so many flyers that I missed seeing most of the people and floats along the parade route. When we got to the end of the line, we pulled off on a side street to let everyone else through.

Knut was formerly a truck driver and rodeo rider and had a lot of stories to tell about his sixty-five years of life while we waited for all of the floats to finish the route and regroup. He had broken just about every bone in his body in the rodeo and started to tell us a few of the gruesome stories. A nephew of his rode up alongside us on his horse and joined the conversation. The nephew had been in the bareback bronc-riding competition for the first time the day before, so Knut started telling him what to expect in the coming years. Once Knut finished talking about being bedridden for months in casts and the hospital bills that took years to pay off, he said he wished he could go back and do it all over again.

There were still a lot of horses on Highway 1 going up and down the streets and plenty of spectators left, so we brought the parade back west. Knut knew half the people at the parade, so we had a lot of visitors as we went up the street. Many of the parade goers had brought their own bottles or were over at the Neighborhood Tavern getting tuned up, so we began to have drunk people approaching us and asking for rides everywhere. Knut asked if I minded staying around while he drove the horses and soon we became a taxi service around Effie. Every passenger offered us drinks, and it did not take long for me to feel the glow from them. Knut kept from drinking too much. He knew the cops, though, so he wasn't worried about them trying to bust him with a DWI, but he said the horses knew when he had been drinking and tried to take advantage of him.

Even when it started to get dark and people were lighting off firecrackers alongside us, Knut kept the horses and wagon under control. There were a few times when the horses got moving pretty fast, and people were wandering up and down highways 38, 1, and 5 oblivious to all of the horses around them, but Knut successfully kept our wagon from injuring anyone.

We parked by the tattoo trailer in front of the neighborhood tavern and sold raffle tickets until the fireworks display started. There was a guy outside drinking with his rooster, and a lot of people were dancing to songs only they could hear. The hitching post outside the bar was full, so new riders coming in had to hitch their horses up to signposts and mailboxes to go inside for a drink. Knut wanted to get the horses home, and I was ready for bed, so we said our good-byes and went our separate ways.

Whenever I visited Effie for the rest of the summer, I received royal treatment, especially at the café where I was treated to free coffee and old bakery goods.

CHAPTER
14

The river pigs, those seemingly fearless men who guided the legendary log-drives in that far-off era before trains, skidders, and logging trucks, fascinated me. Northern Minnesota was the last frontier of white pine logging. As I read about the log drives and put a scene to some of the drives and began to realize some of the waterways were only a few inches deep in places, I had to see the path the logs had taken. After going back to a few of the old drive sites, an unofficial goal of my summer developed to see firsthand where many of the log-drives had taken place. I wanted to kayak everywhere, but I knew I only had a limited number of days. I did not visit some of the many-out-of-the-way lakes. One lesson I quickly learned was that I could portage to most lakes. Around Marcell especially there were several chains of lakes and narrow creeks that connected.

An Eastern branch of the Rice River jumped out at me on the map as I was tracing water routes. I needed to see what that route would reveal. I knew that thousands of logs had come down the Rice River, and that was absolutely mind-boggling since I had been scraping the bottom of my kayak while traversing it. The wing dams built along the Rice River had held up much longer than they had on the Big Fork River, a fact that I attribute to the difficulty canoeists had actually getting through portions of it. With the lack of river traffic, there were not as many people paddling through to grab souvenirs such as spikes and lengths of chain.

The section of the river I tried first was very shallow and choked with lily pads for two miles—not easy paddling by any means. I wished I had gone there in the spring when water levels were higher. It was one place I wrote down on my list of waterways to visit early the next year when the water was higher and there was not so much vegetation.

As I rounded a bend, the smell of decay hit me. A coot floated upside-down in the water. I had been struggling against the lily pads in the hot July sun when I came across the decomposing bird. It seemed a sad sight, but worse than that was the odor. I pushed on hastily and paddled hard. The lily pads were starting to thin out and the water was deeper. Once in open water, I could get away from the sight and smell much quicker.

Despite the dead coot, I continued on. I had not seen that many coots during the summer. There were plenty of mallards around, as well as goldeneyes, buffleheads, and wood ducks, but no live coots. I wondered what had killed the little waterfowl. I had to work my way over several downed logs and pulled apart a few dams that the beavers were just beginning to build up.

Storm clouds started to roll in rapidly when I was about five miles away from my truck. The sky got very dark, and I knew I was going to be soaked. I kept going and figured I would dry out once the storm passed. I put on my poncho and braced myself for the rain. It hit hard for about a half an hour, and then slowly let up.

The sun came out and the sky cleared as quickly as the storm had hit. I was glad I had not turned around. I kept getting farther and farther back and had portaged over several beaver dams when I decided to stop for a while. I was at a wing dam, and stopped to have a porter with the frogs. The leopard frogs surrounded me. Two of them jumped onto my kayak and sat staring at me. When I finished my ale, I moved on, coming across a bridge made with old railroad ties.

Storms had always fascinated me. When I awoke in the middle of the night to a storm raging, I usually stayed up to watch and listen to it. I did not mind being caught in the middle of storms either; witnessing the power of a storm firsthand is something not easily forgotten. I had seen lightning striking trees and the wind whipping treetops back and forth like wheat in a field. Weather was a great mystery, but it was one that I did not mind not completely understanding. I knew enough to know what was happening and why, but predicting what would happen was not of much interest to me. I had not developed any superstitious ways to predict the weather such as many outdoorsmen did. I was happy enough being surprised, and I was not living isolated in the wilderness where I could not escape if things got too bad.

The unpleasantness of soaked clothing was worth being out in the rain, especially when I knew I had a dry set of clothes with me. Once I got back to my camp I had a lazy evening reading and thought it would be a good idea to follow through on my feeling from earlier in the day and go out on open water, I had fought enough lily pads and sweeping brush already to keep me away from it for at least a few days.

Grave Lake was the open water I chose. I went back to Grave Lake with the intention of paddling around leisurely, but I ended up spending a lot of time fishing. Grave Lake fed into Little Bowstring Lake and to the Bowstring River. From there the river went through Bowstring Lake and continued to Dora Lake, where it became the Big Fork River. I toyed with the idea of kayaking to Canada, but when I saw how closed off the Bowstring River was, I decided that staying on the lake was fine.

I found a very old beaver lodge at the point where I decided to go back to open water. Weeds grew through the top of it, and the wood was a dead granite-gray color. I inspected the beaver lodge and noticed the end of a snakeskin near the water.

I got up on top of the lodge and started to look around. The aged wood cracked under my weight. I worked the swamp grasses away and pulled out one whole snake skin. As I examined it, I noticed another one a few feet away. I pulled up the second skin and saw a third, and forth glinting in the sun. I found seven complete skins on the beaver lodge. These were the longest garter snake skins that I had ever seen, they were at least three and a half feet long, and they were all in the same spot. I knew many people who would consider this to be the creepiest thing that they could find aside from a den of live, writhing snakes, but I was fascinated by my find.

As the evening approached, I was out fishing. I decided that my campsite from the night before would still be around when I got back to it. I wanted to fish in the lake more the next morning so I camped on the south side of Grave Lake for the night. That night when I got back from fishing I sat and watched the lightning jumping to and fro in the clouds. I cooked up a can of beans and when I was finished I left the empty can sitting out for the rain to rinse when the downpour began.

The rain from the night before had the fish in a feeding frenzy when I went out fishing in the morning. I had heard stories of fish being in such frenzy that they were biting on cigarette butts. I did not smoke, but I think I could have hooked the fish on a butt that morning. I sang Merle Haggard songs the whole way back across the lake as I returned to camp with a full stringer of fish. The heartbroken ditties were a stark contrast with the happiness and fulfillment that I felt.

The open water had been great to paddle through, but many of the places I wanted to see were not open. I tried to get through a channel that was hopelessly choked with lily pads, but to no avail. I chopped at the pads a bit, then turned around. I had to remember why I chose a lake to paddle. After all, I wanted to be able to paddle with ease.

I pulled the kayak over to Boy Lake and portaged back to Little Dead Horse Lake.

By the time that I reached Little Dead Horse Lake, I was feeling fairly worn out. I explored beaver channels to the north and fished a little. It was very weedy, and there were a lot of submerged trees to hit. I think I bounced off every one of them. I caught a large northern pike and a few smaller, hammer-handle pike. I had enough fish for another huge feast, and after I got snagged on the same underwater tree twice, I decided to filet my meal and head back to camp.

I had a map in my collection that my dad had mailed to me after I had lived in the city for a few years. It showed how to get back to a secret lake. Going to the secret lake was one of my longstanding goals; my grandfather had taken my dad back to it often when he was younger. I wanted to see what the X's marked on the map were for. I had always assumed the X's were either markers for great fishing locations or they places where Old Shovelnose had been spotted.

My grandfather sometimes told a story of a fish named Old Shovelnose that was longer than a canoe and would sometimes surface near fishermen on the secret lake. My dad and uncle had fished the lake and seen Old Shovelnose. When I was younger I had sat enthralled as the three grown men's eyes sparkled like those of children as they told stories about the huge fish. Those who saw Old Shovelnose were supposed to be overcome by a tremendous sense of well-being, and when it swam back into the murky depths of the lake, the other fish suddenly started biting like they would never eat again. I left the lake feeling very well after catching and releasing several decent-sized smallmouth bass. I had not seen Old Shovelnose swimming around out there that time, but I knew I could always go back.

A few of my friends had mentioned a weekend they planned to go camping at the Clubhouse Lake campground months before. I was excited to see if they would actually show up.

The road to Clubhouse Lake had many huge red and white pine trees left standing alongside it. The pine towered over the stands of popple which grew thick around the area. I always drove very slowly through the area so I had more time to observe the beautiful scene I had momentarily become a part of.

While driving a forest road on the way out to Clubhouse Lake, I dodged a mud puddle and went too far to the side. I slid right into the trees next to the road. I attempted to winch out my truck, but the rope secured to the winch snapped against the strain. Being stuck in an out-of-the-way place was nerve-wracking even for me though I had no particular place to be. A slight miscalculation could mean hours or days of work to get a vehicle back onto sturdy ground again. I walked for a couple miles and flagged down a man with a very large pick-up truck. We drove back to my truck, hitched up a towrope, and I was out of the mud and back on the road in a matter of minutes.

After getting unstuck, I took my kayak over to Clubhouse Lake. The campground was very busy with families on vacation, but I did not see any sign of my friends. The lake echoed with kids playing tag in the water at the campground beach. I listened with amusement as the voice of one young boy rose above the fray. It seemed that his sister had pulled his swim-trunks off underwater and hid them somewhere along the shore. I got another laugh when the same kid got his trunks back and then started jumping up and down on the beach, one of the adults yelled out to him, "Did you get a snapper in your shorts?"

Clubhouse Lake is the official head of the Rice River, although creeks connect the river with several lakes further south. I kayaked along the Rice River from the north end of Clubhouse through a culvert and into Mikes Lake. Once through the channel, the river ran through thick bul-rushes and wild rice.

I cut over to East Lake and pulled up onto the island in the lake and looked around. I found a bird's nest and an old mattress frame in the bush-es. It looked like it would make for a nice camping spot, but I still had a lot of daylight left and more exploring to do.

At the far end of the lake, I followed a creek over a few beaver dams and found an area that had recently been clear-cut. There was a lot of potential firewood sitting in the new clearing in the forest. I would be back later. I kept paddling until I reached a gravel road sunken almost enough that I could nearly cross it without getting out of the kayak, but ahead of me I could see three large Norway spruce blown down over the water, so I turned around.

When I got back to the lake, I pulled my kayak up onto shore and walked up to the East Lake Pines. The East Lake Pines was another place where many old-growth white and red pines remained standing. It was not accessible other than by canoe. Private land kept the trees sheltered from most tourists. I walked through the enormous trees and picked up a few of the giant pine cones to compare with cones from other trees. I found a few trees that had been tagged by the Forest Service with numbers as part of a continuing study. As I stared up the trunks, I was reminded that such giant trees had been used for ship masts by the British Navy and were indeed a treasure.

From East Lake I paddled back into the channel and joined back up with the Rice River. I paddled on to Copenhagen Lake and into a large bog on the other side of it. A doe and two fawns stood and watched me as I approached, finally bounding away when I got too close. I continued down the river for a while, but the flies were terrible, so I turned around and headed back to the island on East Lake to set up a camp, and hopefully catch a few fish for supper.

After stocking up on supplies I found another route back to the Rice River by cutting over to Slauson Lake. There were many old-growth pines around Slauson Lake that had been tagged by the Forest Service. The pines towered over everything around. The trees inspired me. They had taken hundreds of years to grow so large. I had only been alive a quarter of a century. The wild rice was coming up on the lake more than anywhere else.

While on the water, I gathered up bullhead lilies to cook later on. When gathering them, I always made sure to only grab lilies that were still closed, otherwise they would be filled with bugs. Sure, the insects were added protein, but I liked to leave them for other animals. There was several northern pike swimming around in the river. I pulled off to the bank to toss in my line, and fifteen minutes later I had two decent-sized pike to eat. The pike are a bony fish, but once I picked the bones out of my teeth they provided a lot of food.

The flies were not nearly as terrible as I continued along the river to Cameron Lake. During the logging era, Cameron Lake was a sorting station for the log drives that took place along the Rice River. Several deadhead logs still floated around the deep, murky lake with the loons. There was an eagle nest on the west end, and the eagles it belonged to were returning from fishing while I floated in the middle of the lake.

I started a fire by the landing and cooked up my pike for a late lunch. No one else was around, so I went walking along the forest road that led to the lake. The road actually shared its route with a snowmobile trail. The trail converged with the road near the lake for a short section of it. The

Cameron Lake snowmobile trail connected with the Marcell Trail over by Highway 38. I had hiked past it on my "long walk."

Stands of popple trees on both sides of the road looked like they had grown up after all of the white pine was cut down. Further up the road, the popple had been clear-cut and was lying in huge piles.

Heavy equipment had brought down the forest. The piles were scaled and the board feet in each log were marked on the butt end. They were dated from the day before. I was amazed. I had been on the lake while the crew had been preparing the logs to be picked up. Soon the trucks would come and haul all the logs to the sawmill, where they would be turned from towering trees into products for the marketplace such as toilet paper.

The dirt roads in Northern Minnesota provided me with great experiences down every one I drove. Obviously a lot of manpower and thought went into planning the roads. I was upset when I came across sections of former gravel road that were being tarred over. These trails through the woods cut down on the seclusion of the forest, but the dust rising in the air behind my truck as I rumbled over the gravel back roads was an affirmation of life.

It was cathartic to focus my eyes in any direction and see trees, lakes, and hills. The roads were not that heavily traveled, but tar inspires people to drive fast and more recklessly than on gravel, and the wildlife along the roads were in more danger. Animals that were moving on because of a fragmented environment would not be back anytime soon. The caribou were long gone from Northern Minnesota, and I could not help but think that if the roads were not in place, there would still be moose commonly seen in the area. The roads allowed me to get to where I wanted to go a lot faster, but I would rather wander on foot and kayak. Hiking and kayaking were activities that gave me time to enjoy what was around me.

Wandering through the forest on foot was similar to kayaking in that it could be enjoyed at a leisurely pace. Any time of year would bring me different experiences and by foot was the only way to actually be able to see everything. All of the birch, maple, popple, oak, elm, ash, and all of the other hardwoods lose their leaves in the winter and leave much to the imagination. In winter the pine tower overhead and give color to the snow covering everything.

Cameron Lake and the Rice River would be freezing up again soon enough, and everything about where I walked would look different. Truth be told, hiking over the Rice River when it froze would be relatively easy compared to navigating it by kayak during a dry summer. Walking over frozen lakes and ponds to get to where I had not been before really brought the changing of the seasons into focus.

The problem with leaving a vehicle behind and floating downstream was that I had to work very hard to get back upstream, especially through rapids. I got back in my kayak and had to paddle upstream. It was not overly difficult in most areas, but when it was very shallow and the water was moving rapidly I had to really exert myself to keep the kayak from spinning around on me and being forced back down-stream. I fought against the current and passed all the blown down trees that I had cut out of the way on my trip north. I thought about the summer before and being stuck inside on beautiful days.

I would drive to the woods to forget it all for a time. I was always reminded when I heard a car or saw another person that I was not alone anywhere I went. In the woods I saw a car pass every fifteen minutes on the gravel roads, while in the city on even the side streets on slow days there were more like fifteen cars per minute. That thought gave me perspective when I felt as if there were too many vehicles around.

When I had been working in the warehouse, my time passed quickly, but I could not stand myself when I thought of all of the time that I spent working for someone else and avoiding my own life. Money was money, to get money meant doing things I did not want to do. Working for someone else made things easier because I avoided the vision and drive to strike out on my own. I figured that all my problems boiled down to laziness, and maybe if I were to stop not trying I would run into another problem. I was comfortable sticking by the old stand-by sin of sloth.

Holding a steady job was a buffer. A steady job meant I was comfortable. I could afford to ignore some of the problems in life with a steady job. I did not have to worry about how much money would be left and when and how I could earn some mammon again. Having a steady job gave me the outward appearance of having my life together and in a strange way it made me feel that I was a part of my city.

Sometimes I felt that I was a part of my community. At times I felt like I was happy with it, but when I would analyze my life at any level beyond the superficial I knew that I was a fraud. Life often seemed so ugly and chaotic, and earning a good living was enough to stave off the depression, but not to get rid of it. I did not want to find out what happened when I tired of the money. I did not have anything else that seemed worthwhile to work for while I was living in the anonymous beehive of the city.

When I was stuck I knew I should be traveling. I wanted to go out exploring, but sometimes what I wanted just seemed closed off. I was fighting off bouts of depression from my dreams, seemingly so distant.

It helped to go out into the forest and clean up debris. I would start a campfire and my mind would feel cleared of all of the confusion and discontent. I would always get depressed again when I would realize that my adventure would end and I would have to go back to doing things that I did not want to do. Forgetting my discomfort for even a few hours was well worth any hardship required of me to be alone in the great out of doors.

In America we're sold the big lines. We can be whatever we want to be, but the luxuries of having everything available mean that many people will never figure out how to get past the struggle. The pursuit of happiness is guaranteed to all Americans, but there is no guarantee that the effort will prove too insurmountable for the realization of the dreams of individuals. I was pained to know that many people did not have any dreams to work toward.

The primal contentment that going to the woods gave me would sometimes last for days, sometimes even until the next weekend.

While in the city I had kept myself sedated with books and movies, music and history. If my mind was spinning I was not busy thinking about my own life, and that was the way I wanted things to be for several years. When it came down to it, living with a mind meant either contemplating existence, or blocking out the question.

The simple truth was that crowds seemed ugly and boring.

My thoughts often seemed ridiculous to me, but I knew what I wanted. Even if no one considered my goals realistic, I still had to follow through on them. I admitted that I sometimes laughed when I heard opinions similar to my own being voiced by others. For a while, I thought that if anyone else was like me, I was not being true to myself. I asked myself the same questions and went through the same bargaining process over and over again in my mind until I finally knew that I had to leave.

Leaving was how I had found myself fighting to get upstream in a shallow river. I knew that no matter how much I swore, I would still be thankful that I had tried out that route once I settled down for the night.

CHAPTER
15

Henry Rowe Schoolcraft, the man Schoolcraft State Park was named after, discovered the true headwaters of the Mississippi River at Lake Itasca. Schoolcraft State Park is located along the Mississippi River southwest of Grand Rapids. In 1832 Schoolcraft arrived at Lake Itasca with his guide, Ozawindib. I drove to Schoolcraft State Park past farm fields and broken forest to visit one day and found the campground quiet enough, so I decided to spend the night there. I was tired out from paddling somewhere around fifty miles already that week.

After waking up the next morning I went out walking on the trails. The park was very small so I actually circled it three times while hiking and admiring the pine. Virgin pines remain standing in the park. The pines were more impressive when I took into account that they were located along two rivers crucial to log drives: the Vermillion and the Mississippi. The Mississippi especially had seen billions of logs driven down to the waiting sawmills in Brainerd, Little Falls, Minneapolis, and St. Paul. It would have been easy for a crew to go out during a drive, cut and limb the logs, stamp them, and push them in the river for extra money.

The Mississippi was calling. It was a bit intimidating getting into a small watercraft like my kayak on a world-renowned river, but after getting in the water, my nervous excitement faded. I found out quickly as I kayaked along the Mississippi that the most difficult part was avoiding boaters zooming along with their motorboats. I could hear the boats coming for quite a ways and knew to get off to the side in case the operators had imbibed a bit too much during their afternoon on the water. Even near shore I could not avoid their wakes. One group of kids sped by in their boat swearing and gesturing wildly at me to get out of their way. The wake they left had me rocking back and forth pretty violently, but I kept from taking on water.

I had never kayaked in any rapids over a class I, so I did not have a spray skirt to keep out the water. If I tipped over a bit too far, I could swamp my craft pretty quickly. Having wakes ripping toward me made me a tad nervous, especially when malicious teenagers produced the wakes.

I paddled up the Vermillion River, and was dripping with sweat. I was only on the Vermillion for about an hour since it was pretty choked with wild rice in places and I did not wish to ruin anyone's crop.

After Schoolcraft I continued toward the headwaters of the Mississippi. I stopped in the town of Cass Lake for lunch the next day. Cass Lake was an early fur-trading post that thrived as a city because of the position it held along the Mississippi River. Cass Lake was fortunate not only because of the nearby river, but the Great Northern Railway line ran through town and connected it to many other towns in Northern Minnesota when it was extended in 1898. The river flows through the namesake of the town, Cass Lake.

It is believed that missionaries had early trading posts around Cass Lake. A fur post was set up in 1760 at the future site of the town, but the post was abandoned in 1763. As the years went by, new operators moved in to fill the void. John Jacob Astor took over the fur trade around the area in 1821 when his American Fur Company bought out the fur post.

The lake itself was originally called Red Cedar Lake, but was renamed Cass Lake in honor of the Michigan territorial governor and explorer Lewis Cass, who led expeditions through the wilderness around Lake Superior and the Mississippi River to survey the land that at that time was part of Michigan Territory. Henry Rowe Schoolcraft was a geologist who went along on the 1820 Cass Expedition. The crew started in Detroit and explored along the shores of Lake Huron and Lake Superior. They then met up with the Mississippi River and took canoes down the river to the land that was to eventually become Iowa. They continued east along the shores of Lake Michigan until returning to Detroit. They had left on May 24, 1820, and returned to Detroit exactly four months later, on September 24, 1820.

As I paddled around Cass Lake, I thought of the Ojibwe living in the area during the fur-trading era and about the role that the Mississippi River played as a route for trade and transportation. The fact that the river flowed south meant that it was much easier to move things from the state than into the state. Early settlers were able to make a living through exploring the natural resources of the state. The falls of St. Anthony in the Twin Cities also make a natural barrier for traveling upstream, it was the only major waterfall found along the Upper Mississippi River. I believe that Minnesota had the most at stake concerning the Mississippi River, being that it not only began in the state, but the river ran more miles through Minnesota than any other state.

The Chippewa National Forest Main Headquarters are located in Cass Lake. The headquarters were built in 1935 entirely out of material from Minnesota. The red-pine logs used for the structure were logged off of Star Island and around Lake Thirteen. The fifty-foot tall fireplace was built from 265 tons of rock gathered from around the state. The rocks pulled to the surface and cracked open by the glaciers as they slowly toured the land were the building materials that also put the geologic history of Northern Minnesota on display. Company 705, the Pike Bay Camp, were the CCC and Works Progress Administration workers who built the headquarters into the impressive structure that the Forest Service calls home. It is amazing to see what Company 705 was able to accomplish under the supervision of Ike Boekenoogen, the carpenter, and Nels Bergley, the mason.

I decided that I needed to explore the western portion of the Chippewa National Forest more the following year when I returned. All along the Mississippi River, the forest was beautiful, but the portion of it that was also part of the National Forest was the most amazing. I loaded up on maps and guides from the Forest Service Headquarters to read in camp before I left town.

The Chippewa National Forest was the first National Forest established east of the Mississippi River. In 1908 Theodore Roosevelt signed the forest into existence, although it was called the Minnesota National Forest until 1928. Nearly 1.2 million acres of land was set aside for future generations to enjoy. The forest contains over seven hundred lakes, nine hundred twenty miles of rivers and creeks, and one hundred fifty thousand acres of wetland. The largest breeding population of bald eagles in the lower forty-eight states makes the Chippewa National Forest home as well.

Itasca State Park was calling me. I knew I would not have time to paddle the entire Upper Mississippi before the snow began to come down again. I had the coming years to accomplish a Mississippi journey, but I at least wanted to walk across the headwaters of the river and paddle for a few miles. Six thousand acres of old growth pine remained in the park.

The parking lot was full when I pulled in. As I expected, there were quite a few people around waiting to walk across the river. I hiked around the park and wished I had come right away in the morning before the crowds started to show up. I figured after six o'clock, I would have a more leisurely time.

As I hiked around, I thought of the early explorers to Minnesota. There is not as much recorded history about the area as I would have liked. Most of the early stories surrounding the voyageurs and lumberjacks were lived out anonymously in the wilderness by illiterate men and women and were lost to history. What history was recorded seemed almost magical when I was paddling along the Mississippi or walking through the same woods that had at one time been wild and uncharted.

CHAPTER

16

August and the heat that it brought led me to seek refuge from sweat by going swimming several times every day to cool off. I used the inner tube I had found at Lake of Isles and a square piece of chipboard for a floating table. I sat on my camp chair in the lakes I visited, unmoving for hours. One of the tricks I used for keeping my beverages cool was soaking a towel in water and wrapping it around the cans or bottles. As the water evaporated, my drink was cooled far below the air temperature. The temperature further north was not quite so sweltering, so I took off to find out where I would end up next.

I chose a road and started driving. The road seemed to be pulling me to the Crane Lake station of Voyageurs National Park. The day I started driving northeast, I began hearing reports coming in over the radio of foul weather on the way either late that night or the following day. The weather reports also mentioned the possibility of tornadoes touching down.

I drove to Bear Lake Campground and almost ran over a couple kids who ran out into the middle of the road while hitting each other with sticks. I got out and hiked to a sandpit where three kids on their four-wheelers were speeding over jumps and taking pictures of each other while the little machines were airborne.

On the Link Lake Trail the gravel road split, and the median was filled with seventy-eighty-foot-tall red pines. After driving through miles of red pines, I pulled into Bimbos restaurant near Side Lake and got a burger, fries, and beer.

McCarthy Beach State Park is located near Side Lake, it was south of my destination, but I decided to head there anyway. I hiked around Side Lake, Sturgeon Lake, Pickerel Lake, and the Sturgeon River on the trail system running around them. There was sand and pine everywhere that I looked.

McCarthy Beach on Sturgeon Lake is a beautiful sand beach. It is the sort of beach that college kids flock to on their spring breaks, but it was hidden away among the red pine of Northern Minnesota. There are many Civilian Conservation Corps improvements throughout the park, including the paths and walls in the beach area.

The Taconite Snowmobile Trail goes through the park, and as I hiked along it, the rocks and hilly terrain reminded me of some of the trails I had been on in Colorado. It was seventy miles along the Taconite Trail from Side Lake to Grand Rapids; another future hike was added to my life list.

I hiked along Snake Trail for a few miles but did not see a single snake. In 1895 the Swan River Logging Company, which was owned by logging men Wright and Davis of Saginaw, Michigan, built a railroad to Sturgeon Lake to transport logs to the Swan River from their various land holdings. From the Swan River, the logs were driven to the Mississippi and the rest of the nation.

Thunderstorm and tornado warnings began to be issued over the radio as I continued toward Highway 65. Storms were heading in my direction. The sky was turning very dark and looked quite ominous. I did not have anyplace to go to get away from the storm. The weather updates kept repeating places I had been since I had left Chippewa National Forest. Bigfork, Scenic State Park, Antler Lake, Bear Lake, Highway 65, and Snake Trail. It seemed that the warnings were following me everywhere I had been in the previous twenty-four hours.

I was driving north on Highway 53 near Orr when the rain finally caught up to me. Hail starting pummeling my truck and bouncing off the highway in front of me. My wipers could not work fast enough to keep the windshield clear. I realized then how badly I needed to replace my windshield wipers. The wiper blades kept coming loose, so I stopped in Buyck to fix them and eat a warm meal. During one of the calm periods in the storm, I stopped again near Minnesota's other Vermillion River to take a brisk hike in the rain.

Reaching the Crane Lake station in the rain and mist was like reaching the end of a continent. I parked and walked to the end of the public pier and looked out over the water toward Canada. The Border Patrol was checking boats pulling into the harbor. The Canadian radio stations had been coming in better than anything else, so I was brought up to date on some of the current news and human interest stories relevant in Manitoba.

I drove back on a gravel road to Vermillion Falls and went for a walk along the river. At one time, stolen timber was frequently being driven over the falls. The men who worked the river had a fierce reputation. The crews had a lot to deal with while keeping the logs flowing over the falls. Whenever there was tension between rival crews or within a crew, bloody brawls would erupt. Rivalries developed, and the alpha males were constantly attempting to live up to the tall tales and boasting they bellowed back and forth to each other. The whitewater rats in charge of the advance of the drive had to be incredibly skilled to keep the logs from jamming up at the bottom of the falls.

I climbed on the rocks, but it was quite slippery, and my clothing was getting soaked rapidly so I did not go too high. I wished that I had calked boots like the river pigs to dig in and retain my footing. I continued back to Johnson Lake through the mud.

Johnson Lake was huge. The lake was hidden away at the end of a four-wheeler trail. All-terrain vehicles were the only way to access the lake aside from portaging and paddling through a narrow creek. The end of the road looked like a parking lot for four-wheeler trailers.

The rain was limiting my movement. I set up a camp among the birch and popple near Marion Lake and listened to the rain pounding on my tarp. The rhythmic pounding soothed me into sleep. I came to after dark with my book still in my hand. The following day, I stayed huddled under my tarp, reading about voyageurs and attempting to stay dry. I packed up in the morning and drove in the rain. I had seen moose tracks near my camp that the rain had not yet completely erased, and I was on the lookout for moose as I kept my speedometer in the single digits.

At eleven o'clock in the morning, the sky looked like nightfall was approaching. The rain began to lessen as I continued down the road, and suddenly the clouds cleared up and the forest lit up. I drove back to check out the Echo Lake Campground. While at the campground, I noticed a rainbow stretching across the sky. According to the most current weather report, the rain would be blowing south, so I drove back to the Crane Lake Station and packed my kayak for a trip.

Crane Lake was very large and wavy. I stayed along shore so I could more readily reach firm ground if I capsized. After passing King Williams Narrows I fully realized that I was floating in international waters. I wondered if I would have to fend off pirates or the border patrol while floating near the water boundary.

The northern border with Canada had just seemed like a formality to me at one time. The border was being actively patrolled. The Customs officers did not play around, as I had witnessed when I first arrived at the Crane Lake Station. During high school, a friend and I had driven into Canada on a day trip just to get a meal, and we returned to the United States an hour later. We told the inspector on our entry that we wanted to look around in Canada. She asked if there was anything specific we were seeking entry across the border for and we told here that cheeseburgers were our first priority. When she pressed a bit more, we told her that we had heard the burgers were better in Canada. Lunch was sufficient reason for us to be let across, without being searched. After September 11th, 2001, that sort of thing could not be done anymore, and it made me feel uneasy being so close to the border even though I was doing nothing illegal.

Private watercraft were not allowed on inland lakes in Voyageurs National Park because of the threat of the invasive spiny water flea being introduced into the inland lakes. I set up camp on Burnt Island for the night.

I had never camped on such a large lake before. It was fairly windy out on the island. The wind sped up during the night, and I crawled out of my tent at three in the morning to watch the whitecaps illuminated by the light of the stars. I leisurely returned to my truck while paddling along the shore for safety against whitecaps. I wanted to get away from the wind. I would continue my adventures in the Superior National Forest.

The Superior National Forest was established in 1909 by Theodore Roosevelt the year after the Minnesota National Forest. The three million acres encompassed in the Superior National Forest cover Northeastern Minnesota from the Boundary Waters up to the Grand Portage Indian Reservation at the tip. The forest borders Canada and includes the Boundary Waters Canoe Area Wilderness, Echo Trail, and the Gunflint Trail. With my kayak along, I was well prepared to enjoy the forest. Over 695 square miles of the National Forest is water and almost half of the eastern lakes of the United States are within the boundaries of the forest. It was overwhelming to visit and decide where to paddle; it would take a few years if I were to paddle all of the lakes.

Trout thrive in the cold northern streams, which crisscross the land through the Sawtooth Mountains and out to Lake Superior. Everywhere I looked lakes and streams waited to be fished and paddled through. The sheer number of lakes and waterways made fishing very exciting. The lakes did not suffer from being over fished like many further south are; the fish are very plentiful throughout.

The Echo Lake Trail was the next section of my adventure. The gravel road wound through the forest uninterrupted. The wildland fire-fighting agencies had landing areas cleared in a few places along the road, so there was a place to land helicopters during fires in the uninhabited forest. I stopped at Lake Jeanette to see the mist rising off the water and opened a can of peaches.

There were three pelicans circling around the rock islands near the landing I paddled toward in my kayak. I ended up following the pelicans half way around the lake. There were small rock islands with cedar and spruce growing up through the cracks that dotted the lake. I noticed a bonfire going on the northwest shore. As it started to get dark out, I began to hear a rhythmic thumping echoing over the lake. I started to paddle toward the fire to see where the sound was coming from.

There was a group of people gathered around the fire. There looked to be at least ten in the group from my vantage point on the water. A woman's voice called out to me and asked if I was friendly. I replied in the affirmative, and several voices yelled out invitations for me to join them. The campers all looked to be in their twenties. The smell, which I assumed emanated from the hookah next to their fire, told me they would be friendly folks.

As I neared the shore, a man who had been playing what looked to be a homemade guitar while two women beat on bongo drums stopped and pulled me up on the needle-covered beach. There was a circle of unoccupied drums around the fire. The rest of the group was spread out throughout the forest when I arrived, but I was told they would be returning within the hour. The group had tents and tarps strung up in the trees and tie-dye flags hanging limp in the still night.

When I got to shore and stretched out my legs, I had food, pipes, and drinks offered to me from all directions. The group and I made our introductions, and I was politely interrogated to be sure I was not there to bust them for any of the numerous infractions they were committing. I assured them that I was a fellow traveler and within an hour I was an honorary member of the Proudhon Tribe.

The Proudhon Tribe turned out to be a group made up of musicians and artists from around the Upper Midwest that got together a few times a year to celebrate the holidays. The holidays that the Proudhon Tribe celebrated were occasions that only the members knew the names or dates of. The tribe was celebrating the festival of summer warmth. I asked where it came from and was told that they created all their holidays to give meaning to their lives. The rituals served to connect the tribe as a community. The members of the tribe saw themselves as social animals. They did not believe in any power higher than themselves. They did not see each other very often, and found that celebrations were more memorable if they created their own mythologies and superstitions to live by. The ceremonies they performed did not involve much other than chanting certain words over and over again and doing yoga near various rocks, trees, lakes, and streams.

The tribe called their camps Temporary Autonomous Zones and declared the ground they walked on to belong to no one. The tree and animal spirits that had inhabited the area for millennia were honored as a pantheon of deities. The members eked out livings through their art, music, and from selling crops that they harvested in their gardens.

The Proudhon Tribe honored me as their guest for three days. I heard many discussions about anarchism and esoteric topics. One night a conversation about the sunken city of Atlantis and lost cultures lasted until the sky began to lighten with the approach of another day. We went for several day hikes around the lakes along the Echo Trail. We hiked around Maude, Pauline, Astrid, Crelin, Picket, and Salt Pork Lakes during our time together. I saw five moose during my time with them also. It was amazing that there were any animals around at all with how many humans were gathered together. I got addresses from the members that had addresses and was invited to come and stay with them for as long as I wanted. The way that they offered was very genuine. I was sure that they would be meeting their entire lives judging by the strong bonds of friendship and unselfish reciprocity each of them displayed.

The Echo Trail was still waiting for me after my meet up with the Proudhon Tribe. I took the Moose River Road and hiked back on a few old grown-over paths. The road passed above the lake, and a narrow spur wound down to the water. I had a picnic at an island on Ed Shave Lake and went fishing for a few hours with no luck.

A cloud of fog moved in as the sky started to darken. The fog moved in quickly, and everything around me was smothered in it. As I eased into camp near Meander Lake, I was completely engulfed. My fire looked blurry as I watched the flames dancing around the burning stumps and brush. An owl was hooting very nearby, and I felt as if I was in another world, isolated from buildings, people, and cars. I felt alone after all of the time I had spent with the tribe, but I was not really lonely.

I drove on to Winton next to visit the town. Winton, next to Fall Lake, is only a few miles East of Ely, but has a distinguished character. It has many canoe outfitters for the BWCA, but the most active business seems to be the municipal liquor store. Most homes have at least one canoe or kayak in their yard, and no matter how run down any of the buildings become they would still have class.

The drive east on Highway 1 was scenic—plenty of trout streams to stop at and attempt to catch the flighty little fish. I took my kayak out on Gypsy Lake for a quick paddle and thought of trout as I went to sleep.

After breakfast I packed up and drove to a pullout along the West Branch of the Baptism River. I waded up and down the river and focused on the riffles and any signs of the little fish. I ended up spending the entire day catching and releasing trout. When it started to get dark out, I decided the best thing I could do would be to set up a camp for the night and finish driving along Highway 1 in the daylight.

Tettegouche State Park was my first long stop along Lake Superior. I hiked back to Micmac and Tettegouche Lakes. I twisted my ankle on the way back, and had to sit down for a while with my boot and socks off. At Shovel Point, I climbed up some of the short cliffs, and I watched the rock climbers with all their gear clambering up the large rocks. I had taken a rock climbing class in college to cover a physical education requirement and did not like it. I loved climbing up rocks, but the emphasis on safety and gear took the fun out of it for me.

I drove all the way up to the east point of Minnesota at Grand Portage while looking for a place to set up a camp for the night. Grand Portage State Park, right on the border with Canada, is named for the nine-mile portage that the voyageurs used to follow with their trade goods through the area. The land the park is on is actually owned by the Grand Portage Indian Reservation and is leased by the state for the park. The park trails follow the Pigeon River, and I was impressed with the High Falls and Middle Falls.

A black bear ran across the path in front of me as I started out on the trail to the High Falls. Camera flashes went off like fireworks as several people stopped to take pictures of the bear.

After leaving the park, I pulled off on a series of rarely used dirt roads. It was dark out, but I felt like driving, so I kept turning off on the spur roads and seeing where they led. Lightning was flashing far off to the east of me. I found my way onto Old Highway 61, which was still partially paved. The potholes along the route had been slowly filled in with gravel over the years until eventually there was no tar left for long sections.

Around one in the morning, I started my drive back to Partridge Falls. There was an old abandoned shack along the Pigeon River that glowed eerily in my headlights. I shut off my truck and went to investigate.

The front door of the shack was resting inside against the back wall with a note nailed to it penned by some type of hard luck case who had spent the night there previously. The signature was impossible to read, but the note was a touch that added to the aura of the place. The shack was missing plenty of boards from the ceiling and would not keep the mosquitoes out. There was a large barrel stove in one corner of the room that looked like a good place to warm up. I was there at the wrong time of year to need it though.

I continued driving on the trail along the river until I reached a depressed spot too muddy along the bottom for safe driving. I decided I needed to turn around and see the rest of the trail on foot. I discovered that I did not have enough room to turn around before the mud hole. I pushed down of the gas pedal and picked up as much speed as I could to get through the mud. I made it and got to the top of a small rise where I had enough room to turn completely around. I again picked up speed going back down the rise, but there was a split second of confusion when a coffee cup rolled under my right foot and got stuck. I was forced to swerve just enough that I ended up sliding into the sloppiest part of the mud pit. I cursed and yelled at the sky as I flung my door open and jumped out to look at the new mess I was in. I knew none of my curses did any good, but it helped to let out my frustrations. I calmed down and worked at trying to get the truck out for a few hours. I tried rocking it forward and back, and then I stopped to shovel the sloppy, wet mud out. I repeated this process over and over again.

As I dug through the mud, I found a log stuck underneath my truck. I had to chop it out with my hatchet as I worked with my elbow in the mud and carefully avoided any glancing blows into the gas tank. There were heavy clouds blocking out the stars, but there was a light above me in the sky as I tried to get my truck out.

The sky had been flashing lightning all night and for a half an hour I expected that a big storm was almost on top of me. The heavy clouds started to dissipate as they drifted across the sky, and I used the moonlight as I walked down to the river to clean the mud off of my skin and clothing. The waterfall and all of the mist rising gave me a sense of déjà vu; the scene when I approached the falls could have been out of a dream.

After cleaning off and putting on dry clothes, I tried to get some sleep in the shack. The mosquitoes were thick and they seemed capable of biting through walls. It was too warm for a sleeping bag, but I needed the protection from bites. I kept it on anyway and started sweating immediately. I was soaked in sweat and could not stop wondering how I could get my truck out with the least amount of backbreaking labor. I was quite a ways from any homes or businesses, and even walking to flag down a truck to pull me out could take a day or longer.

I peeled my sleeping bag off and walked back to the truck as it was getting light out. I started rocking the truck back and forth while taking pauses and pushing sticks under the wheels on each side to make a ramp. I slowly worked my way further out of the deep ruts I had gotten into. The mud had dried out considerably in a matter of hours.

After building the road back up with a miniature version of the corduroy method, I reached a point where I knew I could get out. I pushed into first gear and stepped on the gas. My tires spun, then took hold in the wet earth. As I pulled onto the gravel, it seemed very well maintained compared to the mud pit.

I parked by the shack and walked back to the mud hole. I did not want to be anywhere near the pit with my truck again. I smiled at my change of fortune, and then broke out into laughter as I noticed a leopard frog swimming around on the road. If a road could sustain a population of frogs, it was probably not the greatest place to go out for a drive. I thought of commercials for off-road vehicles where the drivers went to the most remote places, and were shown whipping around through the mud. The commercials made the mud look so glamorous. I was interested in knowing what percentage of SUVs ever actually went off-road. I do not think most new four-wheel drive vehicles would ever see terrain like that, nor would the vehicle owners. I was smiling, but as I looked at my drying, mud-stained clothing, I felt more like the road had been driving on me with dirt caked on from head to foot.

After I got cleaned up, I took a long nap near the river. I woke up and discovered that a garter snake had decided to sun itself about three feet from my head. I asked what it had planned for the rest of the day, and it just slowly slithered away from me without answering. I took that as a cue and went for a slow hike along the route of the voyageurs.

The Grand Portage National Monument is a trail that cuts across the northeastern arm of Minnesota from the former site of Fort Charlotte along the Pigeon River to Grand Portage Bay on Lake Superior. I hiked the nine-mile trail both ways and spent another night camped out at the shack. I noticed many different kinds of birds along the trail. It was deep in the forest in a triangle of land connecting the Pigeon River and Lake Superior by land. It was a fairly uneventful trip.

As I left the following morning and made the meandering drive from Partridge Falls to Highway 61 a Customs and Border Protection SUV drove up behind me. I was tailed for about fourteen miles until I pulled off at a Wauswaugoning Bay overlook, and the customs officer followed me in. I got out to stretch my legs, and the customs officer sauntered over and began interrogating me about why I had been at the border with Canada and why. My truck and I were covered in mud. After explaining myself, I was left alone and was relieved that I did not have to sit around while he searched my truck or came up with more questions for me.

I stayed along the North Shore for a few more days. Driving on tar seemed like being at a go-kart track now. The highway seemed well maintained and it was monitored vigorously. Most of my time was spent lounging around my campfire, reading and playing my guitar. I was very seriously considering trying to hike the entire Superior Hiking Trail—205 miles. Taking out my kayak was too enjoyable to take a break from it for long. I was also wary of leaving my kayak and all of my possessions sitting around for so long anywhere. A hike like that would take a bit more planning than I had been doing for any of my adventures so far. I settled on taking short day hikes and decided that I would try to mark my calendar for the following year for the truly "long walk" along Lake Superior.

Judge C.R. Magney State Park is located southwest of Grand Portage along the North Shore. The Brule River runs right through the park. The waterfalls along the river are the highlights of the park. I hiked to Devil's Kettle and watched water disappearing mysteriously into a pothole as I ate a few apples. As I was reading a book, I watched kids trying to hide from their parents in the cedar above the Upper Falls of the Brule River. I got a taste of the Superior Hiking Trail since it runs through the park.

The feeling that I had been on the move for months was catching up with me. I began to reflect on my summer. As happened every summer around the middle of August, I started to wonder how it had been going by so quickly. I did not have college or a job to go back to in the fall. I only had my truck, my kayak, and a few possessions.

Although I did not intend to, I still ended up hiking along the Superior Hiking Trail for quite a ways as I traveled along the North Shore. My North Shore trip was already giving me inspiration for future trips. I planned on coming back the following year to hike the entire trail and revisit the places I had been already. The extra hiking helped to convince me to not let my goal wait too long for fulfillment.

The Sawtooth Mountains jut out of the earth along the North Shore, especially in Cascade River State Park. The name of the mountain range was definitely an excellent description of them. The mountains dropped steeply on their north slope and were set against the descending Cascade River in the park. Cascade Falls along the Cascade River drops over nine hundred feet in the final three miles before it flows out into Lake

Superior. Watching the falls made me think of Colorado. The winter months were coming. It was already getting colder at night, and I started thinking about heading someplace warm for the winter.

At Temperance River State Park I hiked to Hidden Falls, and then to Carlton Peak, which was swarming with climbers. I worked on my whittling skills with a piece of driftwood I had stashed in my pack. I watched the climbers hauling around all of their gear and using the buddy system to climb.

George H. Crosby-Manitou State Park was nice and quiet. I hiked along the Manitou River and stopped to fish for a few hours. The cedar seemed exceptionally fragrant along the river. I wanted to take a nap there in the shade of the twisted trees.

I pulled into Gooseberry Falls State Park as a tour bus was unloading. I walked very briskly to get out ahead of the pack and then slowed my pace. I went out climbing on the rocks and got a decent hike in without having to scramble around too many people. When I returned to the CCC buildings, the bus was gone, and I had a relatively peaceful time. The castle built by the CCC was especially impressive next to Lake Superior.

I loved the North Shore of Minnesota but I felt that I needed to return to the Chippewa National Forest for the rest of the season to see the things that remained on my to do list for the year.

CHAPTER
17

I drove over to the Effie Cafe and got a bison-burger and fries. There was a lot of talk about Alaska among the tables. A highway maintenance truck and trailer came by and stopped along Highway 1. The driver got out, unfastened some straps, hopped into the huge, shiny, brand-new tractor on the trailer, and drove it down the ramps and onto the highway. He then drove the $80,000 beast up and down the road for a few minutes raising and lowering the bucket, apparently getting the hang of the controls and preparing for a hard day's work.

He finally drove over to two old signposts sticking up next to the Highway 1 sign. He knocked the posts over with the bucket and then got out and tossed them on the trailer. He got back in the tractor and stayed on the road for about ten more minutes, not moving much until a car was approaching, then he backed into the center of the road and blocked both lanes for a moment. He drove the tractor back up on the trailer, secured it, got back into the truck, and continued east. It was inspiring.

There were heavy black storm clouds to the northwest, but I decided to drive over to Little American Falls to say hello anyway. The hill was pretty muddy and treacherous since a storm had rolled through at about 5:00 a.m. There was not much left to it but clay and it was at a ninety-degree angle in some places. At the bottom of the falls was a fiberglass canoe, snapped in the middle but still filled with beer cans; sometimes courage is just not enough.

I stood and admired the canoe for a moment. I wished I had batteries for my camera. The canoe now closely resembled the signs along the river at the falls' approach.

I watched the river crash over the rocks and saw a group of hunters attempting to navigate the path down to the water. The hunters decided better of it and had to settle for photographs of the falls with me standing in their view.

Afterward I drove up the Jingo Lake and Turtle Lake Roads. The maples were incredibly dense along the Turtle Lake Road. The sky was overcast, and it looked like dusk under the tree canopies. The rain held off, but the garter snakes had a death wish as I rode back to camp. I restacked a couple brush piles that had been smoldering throughout the morning while I was on a walk with my .22. I was burning up some of the downed trees to open up the space for pine to reseed. I shot a squirrel back in the pines, piled up some broken branches for a future campfire, and then went under my tarp just as the rain began to pour.

Waking up in the morning, eating breakfast, and picking a place to go out kayaking became my routine for the end of August and into September. I had been going out kayaking on at least one new lake every day and had returned to many to keep my food supply replenished with fish. I went out even on the days when it was pouring. I developed the sniffles, off and on, but fortunately they never turned into anything more than a slight annoyance.

I went to Little Cottonwood, Mink, Racetrack, Lebarge, Blind Pete, Owen, Burnt Shanty, Bee Cee, and Beavertail Lakes for day trips while I island hopped and camped for two weeks on Big Island Lake. Going out to the lakes had become a matter of course. It was something I needed to do. Rolling out of my sleeping bag and scanning my map was an automatic reaction now.

The islands had plenty of wood on them, and my camps were pleasant. The mix of birch, spruce, and cedar made for an inviting, secluded camp.

The nights and mornings were starting to get cold again. The start of September had me spending more and more time cutting up and gathering wood for fires. It seems to me that the biggest differences in temperature between night and day occurs in the autumn. In the afternoon I would be wearing only a t-shirt and jeans; at night I had to bundle up. I actually broke out my parka to wear one night when I slept too deeply and woke with my fire giving off only faint wisps of smoke. When a fire reaches that point and the body is cooled down, the flames seem to make it colder out.

CHAPTER
18

O n my birthday, I woke up with my face covered with pine needles and a blue tarp. Dew was soaking everything. It was how every morning had started out for about three weeks. It kept getting dark earlier and was getting light later and later in the day. The cold was hanging around for a few hours after it got light out.

The animals were starting to get very anxious about something. I had been seeing and hearing skunks every night, and the deer were constantly tromping through my camp. The signs they were giving made a nasty prediction for the weather to come. I was not too enthusiastic about a long, dark, cold winter visiting the woods early.

It had been a Tuesday after all; why would I be anywhere else on a Tuesday? No one realized it was my birthday that day, even though the last week I had been talking about a birthday party my friends were planning to throw for me. This year had already been shaping up to be much better.

I began hearing vehicles and voices a few hours before dark, about a half mile from my camp. The sound carried along the lake, I could not make out lights, so I assumed they were at the bay to the southeast of me. As the music got louder and louder and some of the voices were getting closer, I began to get increasingly annoyed. As I sat and strummed my guitar, I heard a young man's voice say, "Hey, there's a fire up here. I bet it's Davy." I saw two flashlight beams through the brush and knew that whoever was coming was not going to miss my fire.

111

I raised my voice toward the flashlights and said, "I don't know who you are looking for, but I'm pretty sure I'm not them."

The voices stopped and the flashlights froze in place, they turned away and then a girl's voice piped in, "Who are you?"

"This is my camp. Who are you?"

"Are you alone? Can we come over by you?" There was some muttering from a few voices and a pause.

"I guess I could be neighborly. I suppose you're not staying very long?" I knew what high-school parties were like up in the woods. I had gone to a quite a few of them growing up. Apparently the kids were still using some of the same party spots.

"Okay, we're almost there. We can see your fire."

The flashlights approached, and three teenage girls and four boys showed in the light of my campfire.

"Hi." This must have been the girl who had been speaking. "I'm Jen, and this is Annie, Sal, Tree, Rufus, Boner, and Jess." The rest of the group nodded in assent.

"Hello there, I'm Cole." I left it at that and the group just sat and stared at me. They had invaded my camp and now they expected me to entertain them somehow.

Jen, being the only talker so far, felt an obligation to get some kind of conversation going. "So is there anyone else here with you?"

"No, I'm here alone."

"Where are you from?"

"Well, I'm from the area."

"Oh, where do you live?"

"Right here for the moment."

"Out in the woods? Don't you have a house?" The group all looked around at each other, a bit intrigued. I noticed a few of the boys eying the rifle leaning against my truck.

"No, I don't have a house, I'm just living out of my truck, wherever I feel like going."

"So, you're homeless?"

"Well, I guess . . . technically I'm homeless. I don't have an address, but I prefer the term vagrant, it seems more appealing to me."

One of the boys spoke up finally, "You're not going to kill us are you?"

"The thought hadn't occurred to me."

Another girl spoke up, "Well, that's good. Do you mind if we stay for a while? We have beer."

"Well, I guess I don't mind. What are you drinking?"

"We've got Hamm's and Schmidt."

"It's been a while. I'll take a Hamm's." I cracked the can and took a drink. So, now that I can see you all, who is who here?"

They spoke up one at a time now as they found places to sit. "Jen . . . Annie . . . Rufus . . . Jess . . . Tree . . . Sal . . . Boner."

"Nice to meet you, I haven't had company in a few weeks."

Boner spoke up. "So, what do you do out here?"

"Explore . . . enjoy my time . . . live, I suppose you'd say."

Annie spoke up next. "Don't you get lonely? Don't you have a girl-friend or a wife or something?"

"I haven't been lonely yet. No, it's just me."

Tree decided to get a few words in. "Hey, I have a kayak too. Do you go out very often?"

"Yeah, I average about a lake a day around here. We do have over a thousand in the county. Do you go out much?"

"I went a couple times this summer. My parents like to take trips to the North Shore and do the big lake."

The kids were all seniors in high school. They were concerned about college and about what they were going to do with their lives, and like most kids they really had no clue what they wanted to do.

"So you don't think college is worth it?" Tree asked.

"It can be. It just depends on what you want to do with your life. It's a good time. It's a few years of buffer before you end up in the meat grinder. I have friends that went through it and who really seem to be enjoying themselves and their careers. It all comes down to priorities really, and what you expect out of life."

113

The kids all seemed to agree. They were a lot different than kids from the city. They were not really career minded to begin with. It helped that there were not many jobs in the area that they could just sit back and get lazy doing like what was found in the city.

Just by living in an area where families really had to work hard and be self-sufficient set them above the rest for survival in my eyes. I thought to myself about city kids and how many of them started thinking about colleges and careers when they first got into high school. They seemed to know so little. It was a bit of culture shock for me when I first moved to the city.

Jess said, "Yeah, the guidance counselor at school laughed at my mom when she asked him about me going to St. Scholastica in Duluth. We're not really expected to do anything with our lives up here. Not to brag, but I got a 31 on my ACT test, and they don't do anything to prepare us for it up here. We just get the practice booklet, and they offer a study period. I have a cousin from Burnsville who takes advanced classes in school. We don't have anything extra up here for smart kids."

Tree jumped in, "I hate to say it, but cities kids are always going to have a lot more opportunity than us. They've got big sports teams, and good classes, and lots of jobs—"

I cut him off. "Most of the kids from the cities are behind you. High schools are just a big fashion show. It seems like none of the kids know how to read, and they don't have anything interesting to say. They live boring, protected lives where their only hardship is getting grounded and not being able to go to the mall on the weekend. Unfortunately those advanced classes that are not available up here and the programs that the schools can't afford mean something on applications, and that same kind of thing matters later on when you are writing resumes.

"Everyone from up here has to try harder, but when you break through, you're that much stronger and better a person for the adversity you had to fight against. Where you grew up, to me, the fact that you grew up in Northern Minnesota, means that you have a lot of knowledge about how to stay afloat and that you should stand out, not that you don't matter because you never had the opportunity to join some club and get a certificate.

"I'm not much older than you, but I can guarantee that in a few years you're going to realize that none of what they have is really an advantage. Knowing yourself is the only way you'll ever be successful."

"You're not successful though, and you seem to know who you are." Annie said.

"I beg to differ, I feel more successful now than I did when I would get a raise or a bonus check. Money doesn't mean success. I know a lot of yuppies, and even though they have a new car parked in the driveway, they always feel like garbage . . . totally worthless. It gets me depressed to think about it really."

"I wouldn't want to live like you are," Jen said.

"Well, everyone's different. I'm sure it's harder for you to see the positive things about living up here since you grew up with it. I was the same way for a while. I know it is cliché, but, 'the grass is always greener,' at least until you've tried it. You can only make your decision then. Even if you all move to the Cities, I'll bet you'll really start to miss it up here. It's not the same when you have a neighbor twenty feet from you at all times, or when you're stuck in a shoebox apartment. It'll be fun for a while, but you let me know in a few years how you feel."

"Did you go to a good school?"

"As far as schools go, it didn't really work out for me. I never found a job in my field, although, I never really had a field to begin with. You never know. Maybe I'll really start to miss the Cities in a year or two and give this all up to rejoin the race. I don't believe in absolutes. Things are always changing, but this feels right for now. I would have been caging up a part of myself that was howling to get out if I had stayed.

"I think you have to let the enthusiasm die down from doing something you want before you can say for sure whether you'll keep the same dream. There was a time when I thought I would be playing in punk rock bands until I died, and I'd see the world from a tour van. I guess I kept part of that dream."

As it got later, my guests began to make their way back to their party. Annie lingered behind everyone and asked if I wanted to join them, but I told her I was happy where I was. They told me they would be back the next weekend if I wanted to come out. I was not used to talking to so many people.

I had not become a responsible adult yet, at least not with the definition, as I understood it. I may have been living out childhood fantasies, but I felt too old to be partying with high school kids.

CHAPTER
19

The Rice River was no longer a mystery to me, but after kayaking some-where around one-hundred lakes that summer, I decided I should return to the Big Fork River and explore it as it wound from Dora Lake to Canada. Although it was a low-water year, I figured I could portage any sections too shallow and explore the whole river before the snow and ice of winter returned. I planned on paddling the river one section at a time. On the calm stretches, I could double back to get my truck and drive to the next access, and I figured that on the bad sections I would be safe enough stashing my kayak and hitchhiking back to my truck. I started out by kayaking from Dora Lake to Highway 14, but then the weather turned cold, and there were not many daylight hours when there wasn't drizzle in the air at the very least.

With the weather being generally unfriendly for a week or so, I was not sure how much I would actually be able to paddle while I had my morning coffee and looked over area maps. I had serious doubts that I would be able to paddle the entire river while faced with the cold snap. I wanted to keep getting out on the water, so I went back to kayaking on small lakes. I went out and returned to camp to change into dry clothes and enjoy my fire. I had to keep rotating firewood to keep a dry supply.

I moved things around in the back of my truck and packed all of my extra clothing and blankets around the side of the box so I had a well-insulated sleeping quarters. When the temperature really dipped, the time of year and the limited number of days left to enjoy open water make selecting my destinations even more difficult.

When I went back to the river, it was very cold out. I put on my wool pants and wore a fleece under my sweatshirt for our reunion. In the place of breakfast, I brought along a few handfuls of pistachios, a can of baked beans, and my canteen. I actually brought my camera with me, which was a rarity since the inside of my kayak got pretty wet by the end of the day with no spray skirt.

I drove over to the Hafeman access and unloaded. I left my can of beans in the truck, and started paddling upstream. A bald eagle was guiding me along for the first quarter mile. The sky was very overcast, but the water was the calmest I had seen it. I did not scare up any deer along the banks, which was very odd. The ducks, geese, and coots were around every bend, however.

I paddled to Hauck rapids before getting out to stretch, and I decided to shoot through the wildest part a few times and portage back for a bit of excitement. I managed to avoid every hidden rock, which was fairly lucky since the water level was very low. I ate my pistachios and watched the leaves swirling downstream from a perch I had crawled out to on a large ash tree leaning over the rapids.

I realized when I was above the rapids that the batteries in my camera were dead. My rechargeable set was drained also. It was a typical occurrence whenever I got a few miles away from signs of humans, so I was not overly surprised or angry. I knew that if I brought it with me more often, I would probably remember which sets of batteries were dead.

I continued up to the Highway 14 Bridge and turned back. I was getting fairly hungry at this point, but I was going downstream now, so it was not so much work. I found some sulfur shelf mushrooms on the banks, but when I broke them apart, they were wormy—I did not have a frying pan along either so they did me no good.

I had three otters keeping me company on the trip downstream. They kept popping up in front of me, and they would occasionally bark and continue on. The otters sometimes hop through the water like dolphins, and these three did it continually.

There is a large portion of the Canadian Shield exposed along the river, and I stopped on an outcrop of it to stretch my legs. I climbed on the rocks and worked the kinks out of my back before I got back on the water.

I found a minnow bucket and enough waterlogged lumber to build a small shack along the way. I usually passed up the lumber because it is too unwieldy to paddle with. I gathered plenty of fresh beaver wood for building bookshelves and fashioned a rack on the bow of the kayak to carry all of the wood. I had a tendency to collect quite a bit of it on each trip.

It was six o'clock by the time I got back to my truck. In all I ended up paddling sixteen miles. I did not see anyone else on the river, and there were only a few beer cans along the way. It was a fine trip and gave me hope for the rest of the autumn.

The temperature had reached freezing at night, but during the day, it was still fairly warm out on the river. I was wearing several layers and never had to shed any. I did some fishing as I floated and watched the banks for wildlife.

I had my camera with me and took some pictures of the river as I floated down it. It was a very easy trip until I reached Rice Rapids. The river had been getting higher since September, but it was still fairly low, so there were a lot of rocks to avoid—and a lot that were scraping at the bottom of my kayak. I only had seventy-five to one hundred yards of rapids left and there was nothing jutting out of the water, so I lowered my paddle, stretched my legs out and let my guard down as I rounded the last corner. I was figuring on enjoying the last little rush. It was a very stupid mistake.

I hit a series of staggered rocks on both sides of me that got the kayak rocking. As I flailed at the water, I hit another rock that turned me sideways and water rushed in from upstream. I lost my grip on the paddle as I rolled out and tried to keep hold of the kayak. The kayak got turned around, and I floated through the rapids with it as I bounced off rocks and tried to gain my footing. At the end of the rapids, I stood up and dragged the kayak over to a huge boulder on the riverbank.

The first thing I did after I climbed out of the water was check for my camera. I lucked out, and the camera case had stayed in the kayak, although everything else that had been in front with me had washed out. I pulled out my camera and dumped the water out of it. I looked across the river and downstream to see if anything was hung up that I could get to but didn't see anything. My paddle, fishing pole, gloves, canteen, bug spray (one of the things I never bothered taking out), and the soda I had been drinking were all gone.

I wrung out my clothes and put them back on, I was very happy to be wearing wool pants, since wool will keep a body warm even when it's soaked. The sun was out and the boulder I was sitting on provided a good place to soak up the rays and keep a bit of heat in. I had banged up my shins, hurt my tailbone, and my lower back had taken a beating coming down the rapids. The adrenaline rush helped, but I could still feel the pain coming on.

The matches I had with were soaked, so a fire was not very practical. The air temperature was still forty to fifty degrees out, so the cold was not unbearable, but a cool breeze had been blowing. The cold was working its way in, and unfortunately my body had never regulated heat very well when I was in the water. When I would go swimming for any length of time, I usually end up with a cold. What I considered to be "any length of time" was over an hour for me.

I checked behind my seat and was glad to find everything was still there, including the voyageurs cure: a flask of rum. Rum will heat a person up quickly and quell the panic after mishaps like ending up swimming in a river in October. Voyageurs often had only their rum to keep them warm after everything ended up in the river. Using flax and a striker is not the fastest way to build a fire. If it has been raining or snowing, using flax and a striker took a miracle to get a fire started.

I sat on the boulder and collected my thoughts. I remembered the last time I had fallen in the water in October. I was probably ten or eleven years old and was back at a beaver dam in Potato Creek with my dad. I had been climbing on the beaver dam, and I slipped as I was getting back into the boat. I fell backwards into the loon shit, the murky black water/sludge

120

commonly found in back bays and creeks near beaver dams and lodges. My clothes were completely soaked, so my dad gave me his jacket as we hurried back down Potato Creek and across North Star Lake to our vehicle. The ride was long and miserable. By the time we got back, I was shaking uncontrollably. I took off all of my clothes and jumped into bed, and then about twenty blankets were piled on top off me. I shivered until I was warm again. I remember feeling cold for about a day after that.

I knew I could either leave the kayak and walk to the nearest road or just float down the river a few more miles to the bridge so I would not have to abandon everything. I dumped the rest of the water out of my kayak and set it down along the riverbank. I found a stick for navigation and to use in the hopes that I would see a few of my possessions along the way and would be able to work my way close enough to them. Navigating was easier when paddling with my hands, so I did not do much poling with the stick. I kept remarkably straight. The current tended to spin my kayak around in the river when I was not paddling. In a few places where the current picked up, I pulled myself along the bank to stay straight. In the end, I reached the road without incident.

I stashed my kayak under the bridge and walked to the nearest house to ask for a book of matches. The nearest house was a large wood cabin. An elderly woman answered the door. She told me she had soup on the stove and invited me inside to warm up. She was living alone after her husband had passed away the previous spring. She gave me some of his clothes to wear and told me to keep them.

We talked for an hour. Her parents had homesteaded the land. She had not wanted to leave when they died. She still had a few head of cattle on her ranch that kept her busy. After delivering her abbreviated story she said she could not stay awake any longer.

She offered a spare bedroom to sleep in, but I politely turned her down since I had my kayak and all of my gear down under the bridge and did not want to be away from it for too long. I made a small campfire in the woods by the bridge and sat with my kayak watching the river for my paddle floating down it.

The next morning I caught a ride back to my truck. The man who stopped was up at his summer home. He was a retired schoolteacher. He had skipped picking blueberries with his wife to go out for a drive. He treated me to lunch at the Backwoods Grill in Bigfork, and told me where to find him if I got lonely. He started to pull away, then stopped and rolled down his window. He offered up two of his old canoe paddles to fashion a new paddle for my kayak. I hopped back in his truck, and we went and rigged up a new paddle for me with a generous portion of duct tape.

Two days later, I paddled back up the river to where I'd fallen in. I scanned the banks and snags as I went up and down stream. I found quite a few boards, a broken dock. I had chest waders with me and walked in the river and recovered a soda can, my right-hand glove, and the can of bug spray, but I didn't find the two most important things: my paddle and my fishing pole.

It was good to be able to see what was below me in the rapids as I paddled. Going through rapids, there isn't much to be seen underneath the water since it is so riled up and there's no time to focus. Being able to tell where the submerged rocks were from the way that the water was moving over and around them was a very handy skill to possess.

I knew I needed to keep traveling as long as possible. The weather was very nice for the first mile of my paddle rescue trip. I had been floating along leisurely and scanning the banks when it began to sprinkle.

I set up a make-shift fishing pole and began trolling. There was a muskrat out in front of me as the rain picked up. I trolled for about a mile, and something big took my line. I fought it for about a minute before my line jerked toward the bank and snapped. I would guess there is a muskie swimming around now with one of my minnow spoons adorning its lip. I decided I didn't want to take the time to tie a new lure on while it was pouring, so I gave up on having fish for supper.

A spike buck was drinking on the bank, and instead of bolting away when I approached, it got curious and walked along the river and watched me until I got to the next bend. The rain slowed to a drizzle about a quarter-mile past the County Road 42 Bridge, and I had a chance to tie on a new lure and toss in my line again.

Three otters were barking at me and following my progress. A bald eagle began circling above my new crowd, and then continued flying along the river going upstream. The otters lost interest, and the rain began to pick up again.

I found a collapsed cabin and stopped to investigate. There were still many pots and pans rusted through and a lot of odds and ends from long ago. I left them for the next visitor to see. I cleaned up the beer cans that had been left by other curious river rats.

As I was within about a mile of the Highway 1 Bridge, I saw twelve trumpeter swans along the river. Half of the swans flew off the river and circled and honked for about five minutes until the rest of them decided to fly away also. The swans make quite a bit of noise when they are in groups. A kingfisher was swooping along the banks, and an osprey flew overhead. With all of the avian activity, it obviously would have been a great stretch to fish. Quite a few deadheads floated in the water to steal my lures, and I did not feel like stopping to cast.

I reached the rapids by Highway 1 and a short way into them got hung up on a rock and spun around. The beginning of the rapids turned out still to be very shallow, and I was not very happy with the beating the bottom of my kayak was taking. I scanned the sweepers along the banks for my lost paddle, but only saw branches and deadheads. I found a deep channel and stuck with it until I passed under the bridge. I hit some deep spots, and the water curled over the bow, but I wasn't swamped. Getting swamped did not matter much at that point, since I was soaked from the rain anyway.

I had been paddling hard and had only stopped once because of the rain. I continued downstream to get some more exercise and to see Chief Busticogan's old site. I found a camp pad floating in the river, but would have preferred to find my old paddle. I paddled up Deer Creek until it was blocked and went downstream farther. There had been a logging camp up Deer Creek over a century before. A farm camp had supplied food for the lumberjacks while they worked during the winter months.

The weather turned from the steady heavy rain and distant thunder that I had been paddling in for a few hours into a torrential downpour with lightning flashing overhead constantly. I had a battle ahead of me to get back upstream through the rapids, and I cursed the gods for the trial they were putting me through.

I reached a few spots where I was only able to make about an inch of progress for every ten strokes. My arms began to burn. I was very proud of myself because I made it back to the landing without taking any breaks along the bank.

I looked around for what afforded me the most shelter from the rain and settled on a Norway spruce near the road. I sat in my kayak under the tree after dumping out all the water and opened a soda as I watched the lightning. My clothes steamed as I cooled down from fighting against the rapids.

A lady pulled into the landing and stopped to ask if I needed help. I told her I was fine and took a sip of my soda as the rain dripped off the rim of my hat and lightning flashed across the sky. She was not quite satisfied with my answer and continued to look at me from her car. I was glad for her hesitation and asked her to wait a moment while I pulled out my dripping bags from inside the kayak and loaded them into her trunk. I stashed the kayak back in the brush and was on my way back to camp, defeated again.

After having two very cold trips, I decided that, if I was going to continue living out of my truck, I should make things a little easier on myself and migrate with the seasons.

I've been thinking about going to Colorado for the winter again. I can always come back to Northern Minnesota next summer. I'm young after all. There'll be a few years before the money runs out. Southwestern Colorado resonates in my mind as I look at all the wet layers of clothing I've peeled off and hung up. They're now hung steaming next to my fire.